Have you read all these books by
Rachel Renée Russell?

DORK DIARIES

Dork Diaries	TV Star
Party Time	Once Upon a Dork
Pop Star	Drama Queen
Skating Sensation	Puppy Love
Dear Dork	Frenemies Forever
Holiday Heartbreak	Crush Catastrophe

How to Dork Your Diary

OMG!: All About Me Diary!

THE MISADVENTURES OF MAX CRUMBLY

Locker Hero

Middle School Mayhem

Rachel Renée Russell

DORK diaries

BIRTHDAY DRAMA!

With Nikki Russell and Erin Russell

SIMON AND SCHUSTER

First published in Great Britain in 2018 by Simon & Schuster UK Ltd
A CBS COMPANY

First published in the USA in 2018 as *Dork Diaries 13: Tales from a Not-So-Happy Birthday* by Aladdin, an imprint of Simon & Schuster Children's Publishing Division.

Copyright © 2018 Rachel Renée Russell
Series design by Lisa Vega
The text of this book was set in Skippy Sharp

The right of Rachel Renée Russell to be identified as the author and illustrator
of this work has been asserted by her in accordance with sections 77 and
78 of the Copyright, Design and Patents Act, 1988.

1 3 5 7 9 10 8 6 4 2

Simon & Schuster UK Ltd
1st Floor,
222 Gray's Inn Road
London WC1X 8HB

Simon & Schuster Australia, Sydney
Simon & Schuster India, New Delhi

A CIP catalogue record for this book is available from the British Library.

HB ISBN: 978-1-4711-7276-2
Export PB ISBN: 978-1-4711-7315-8
eBook ISBN: 978-1-4711-7278-6

This book is a work of fiction. Names, characters, places and incidents are either
the product of the author's imagination or are used fictitiously. Any resemblance to
actual people living or dead, events or locales is entirely coincidental.

Printed and bound by CPI Group (UK) Ltd, Croydon, CRO 4YY

MIX
Paper from
responsible sources
FSC
www.fsc.org   FSC® C020471

Simon & Schuster UK Ltd are committed to sourcing paper
that is made from wood grown in sustainable forests and supports the Forest
Stewardship Council, the leading international forest certification organisation.
Our books displaying the FSC logo are printed on FSC certified paper.

www.simonandschuster.co.uk
www.simonandschuster.com.au

www.dorkdiaries.co.uk

HAPPY BIRTHDAY TO MY
DORK DIARIES FANS!

I hope your birthday is as special
as you are ☺!

OMG! MY BIRTHDAY PARTY IS BEYOND AWESOME!

SQUEEEE ☺!

Just imagine a FABULOUS and FUN bash at the Westchester Country Club with a band, DJ, all-you-can-eat pizza, ice-cream sundae bar, two hundred of my closest friends, my loyal BFFs, my adorkable CRUSH, and a humongous birthday cake.

Everything is SO unbelievably PERFECT, I need to pinch myself to make sure I'm not dreaming. OUCH!! That hurt! (I just pinched myself!)

The GOOD NEWS is that not even my mortal FRENEMY, MacKenzie Hollister, can RUIN the most AMAZING day of my entire life ☺!

The BAD NEWS is that I was totally WRONG about the GOOD NEWS ☹! . . .

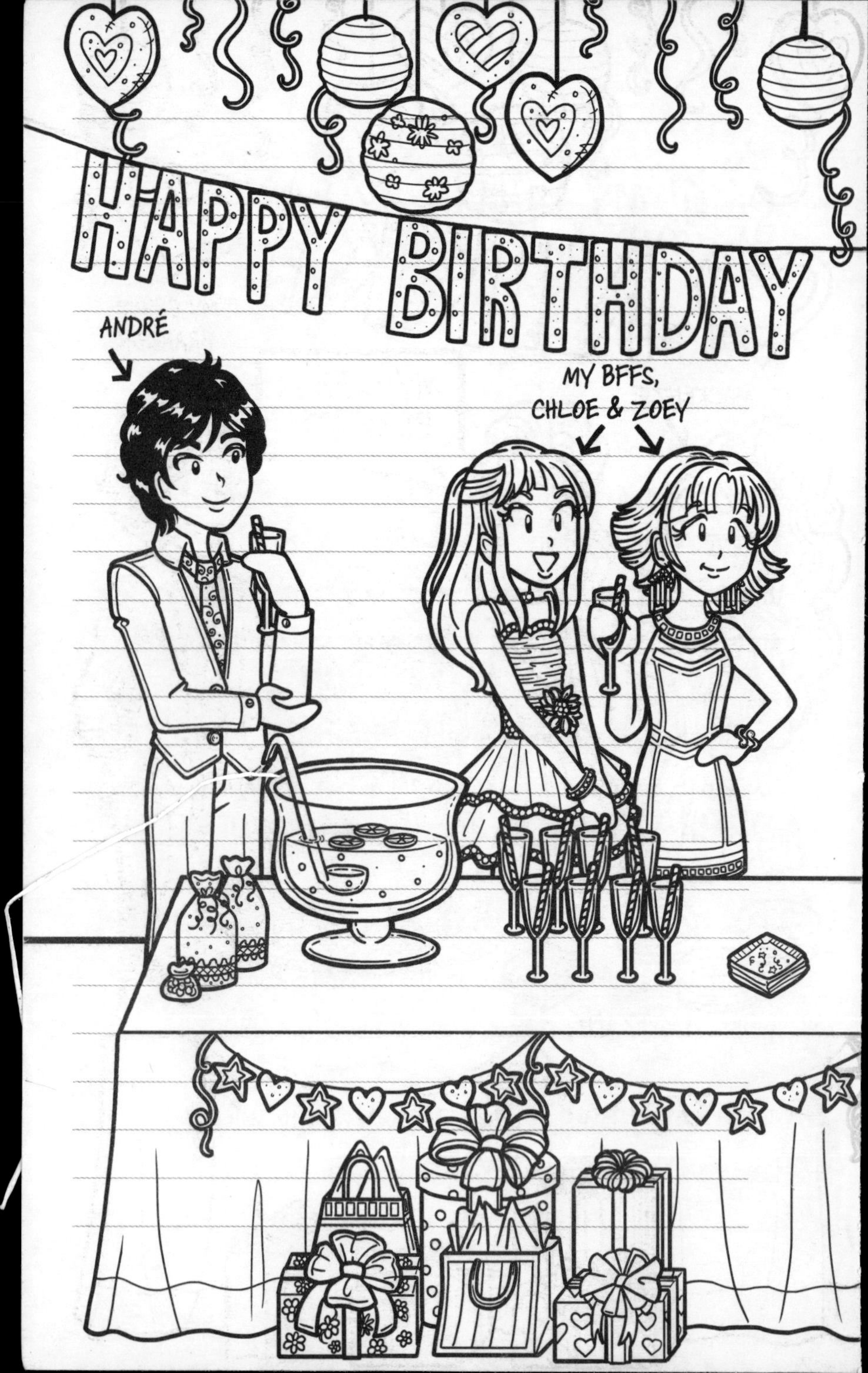

HAPPY BIRTHDAY
ANDRÉ
MY BFFS,
CHLOE & ZOEY

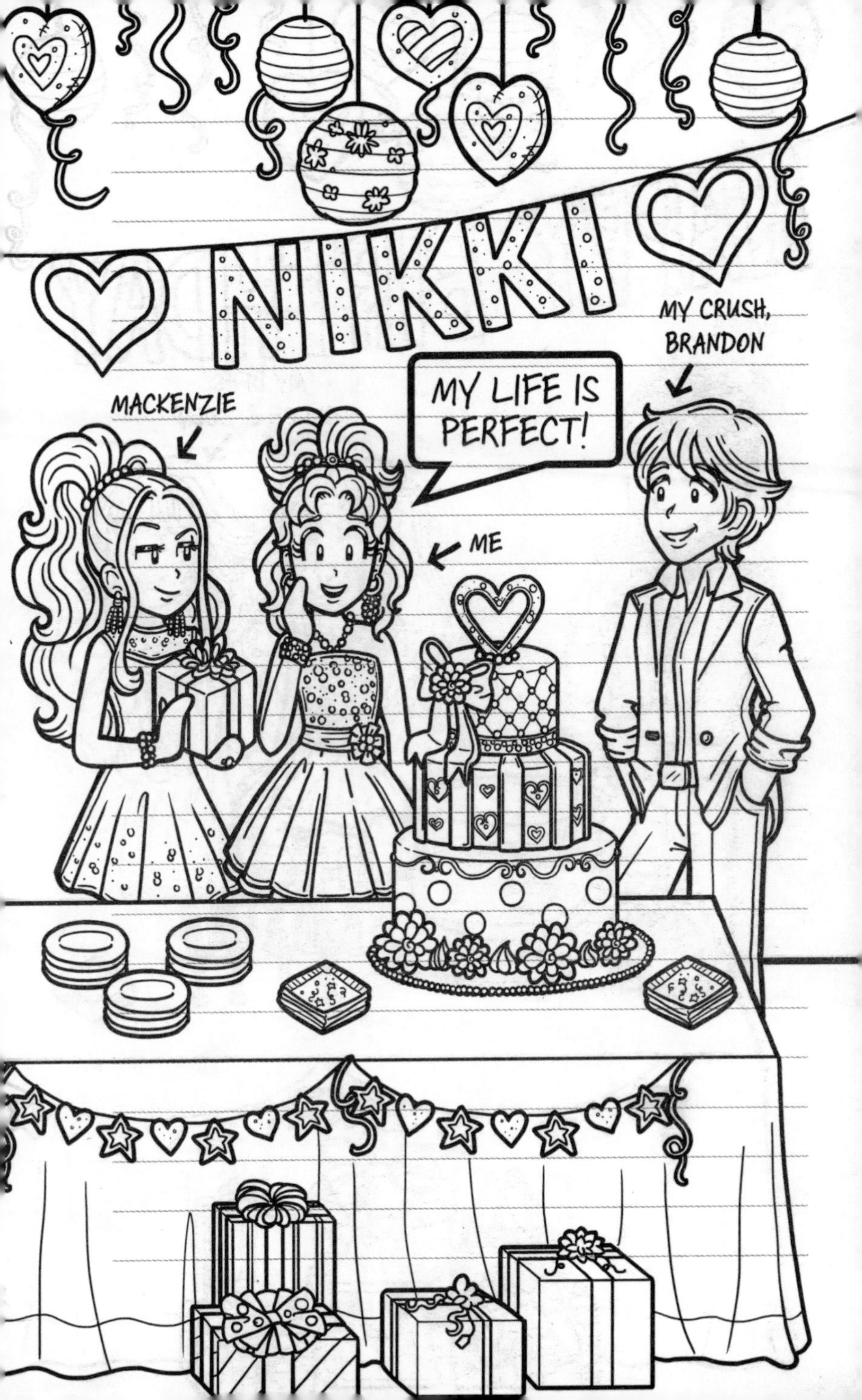
NIKKI
MY CRUSH, BRANDON
MY LIFE IS PERFECT!
MACKENZIE
ME

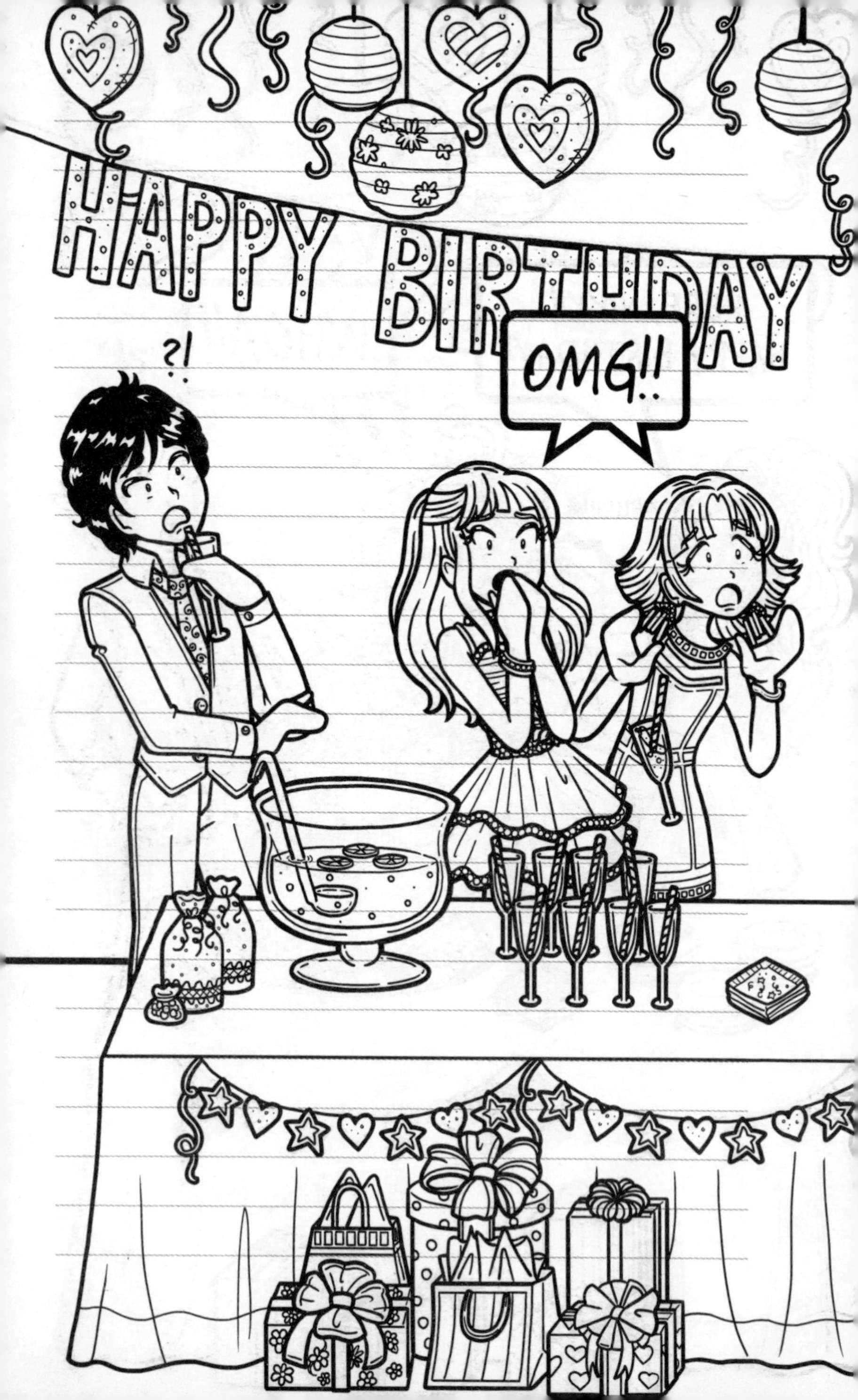
HAPPY BIRTHDAY
?!
OMG!!

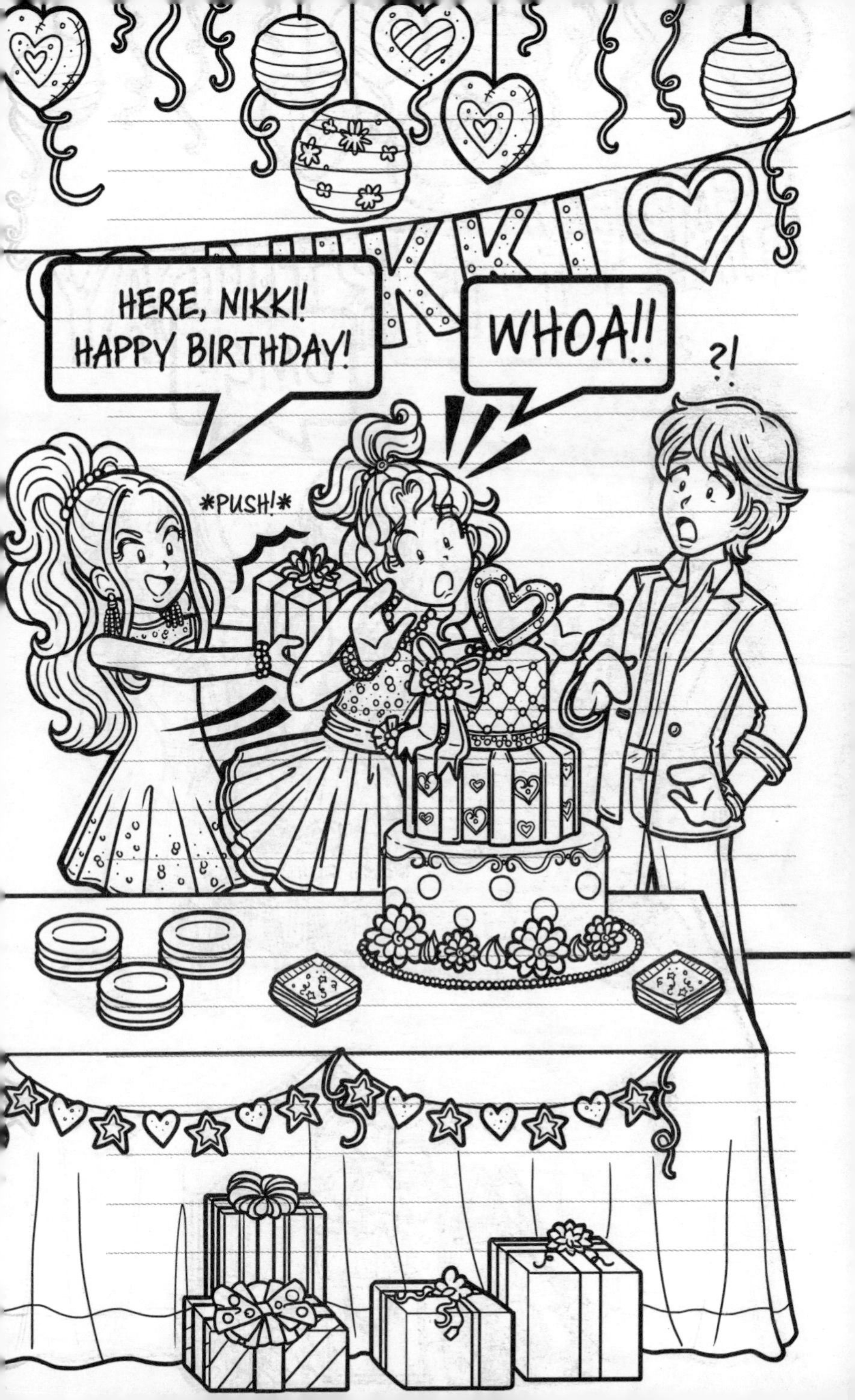
HERE, NIKKI! HAPPY BIRTHDAY!
WHOA!!
?!
PUSH!

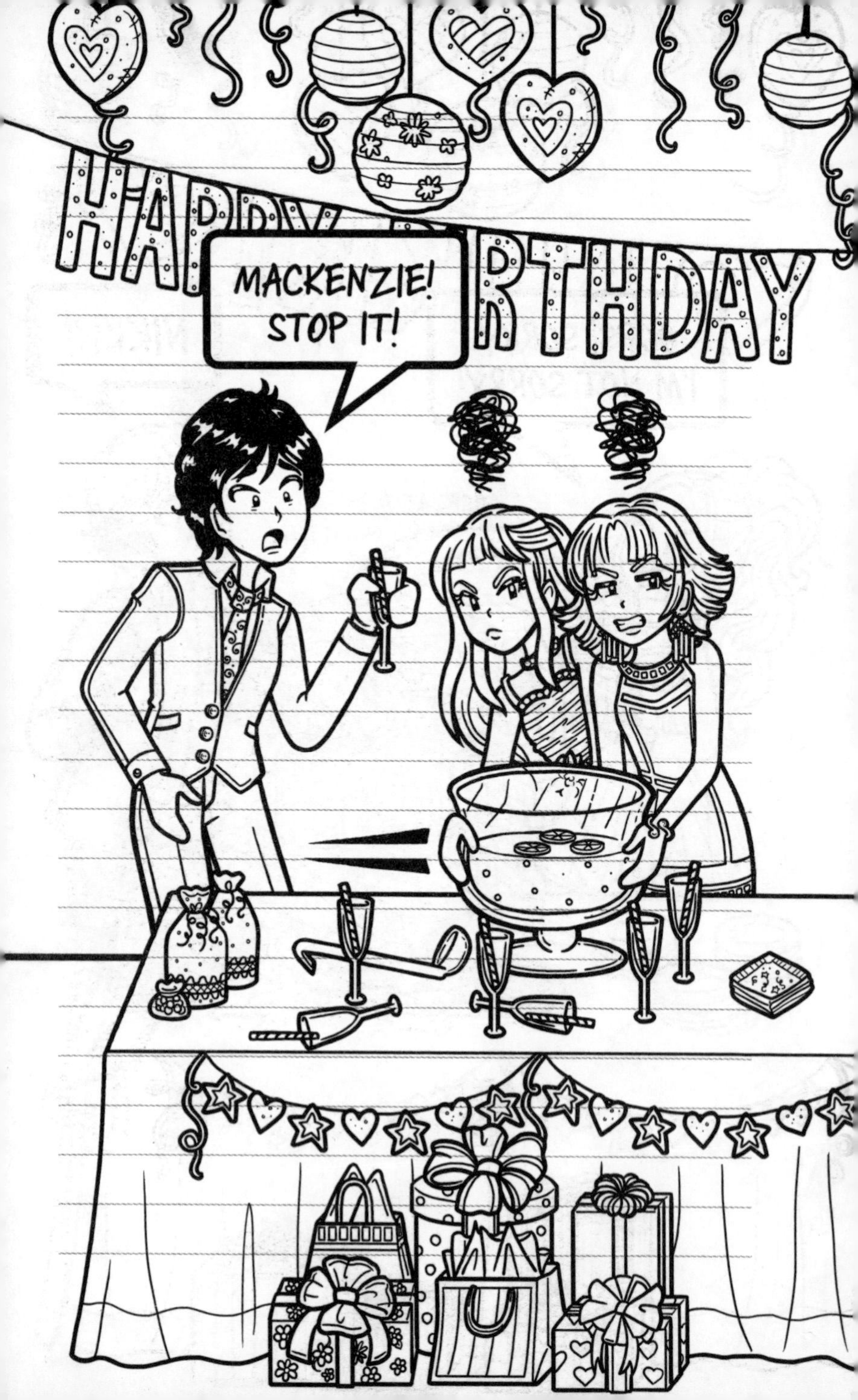
MACKENZIE! STOP IT!

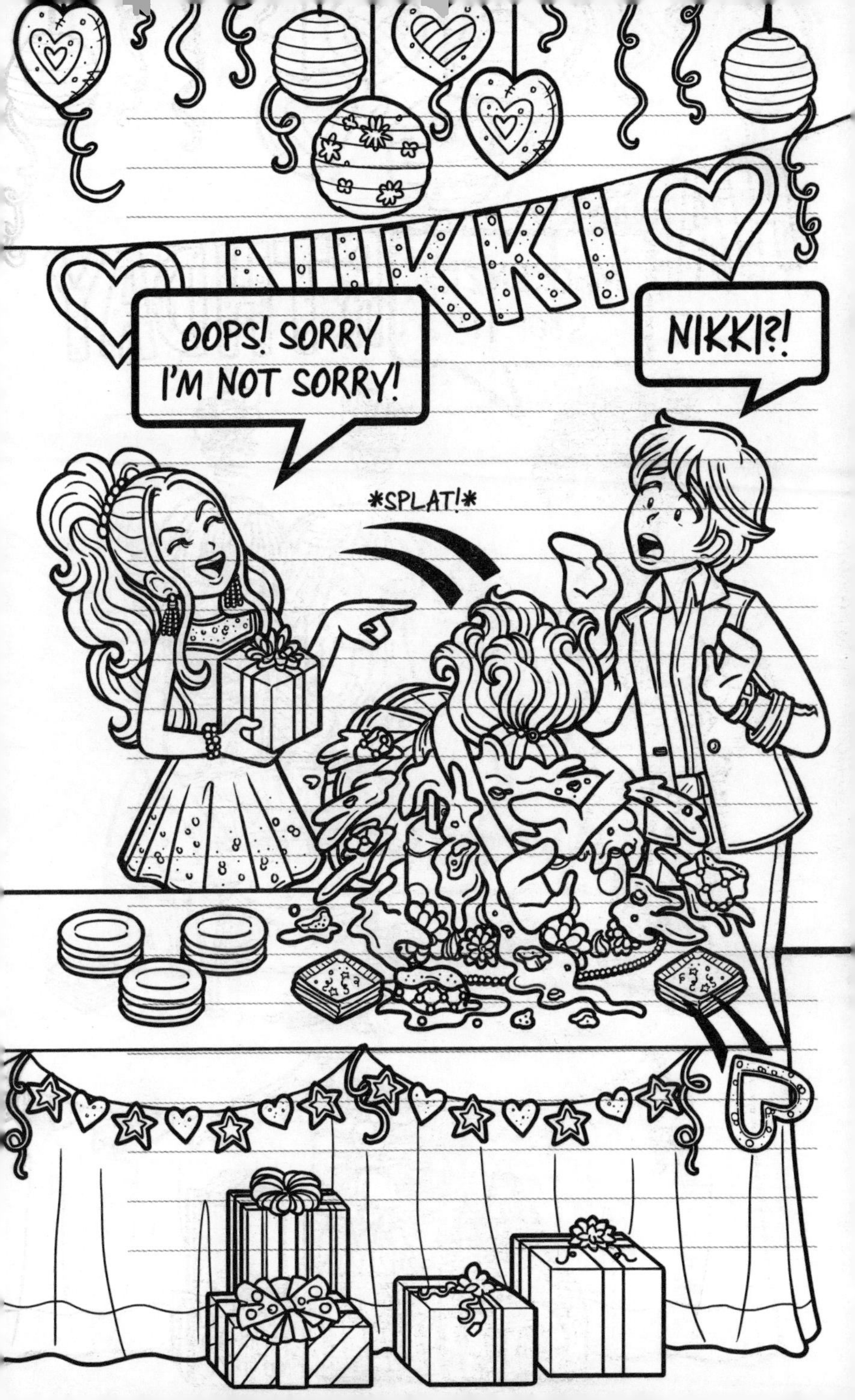
NIKKI
OOPS! SORRY I'M NOT SORRY!
NIKKI?!
SPLAT!

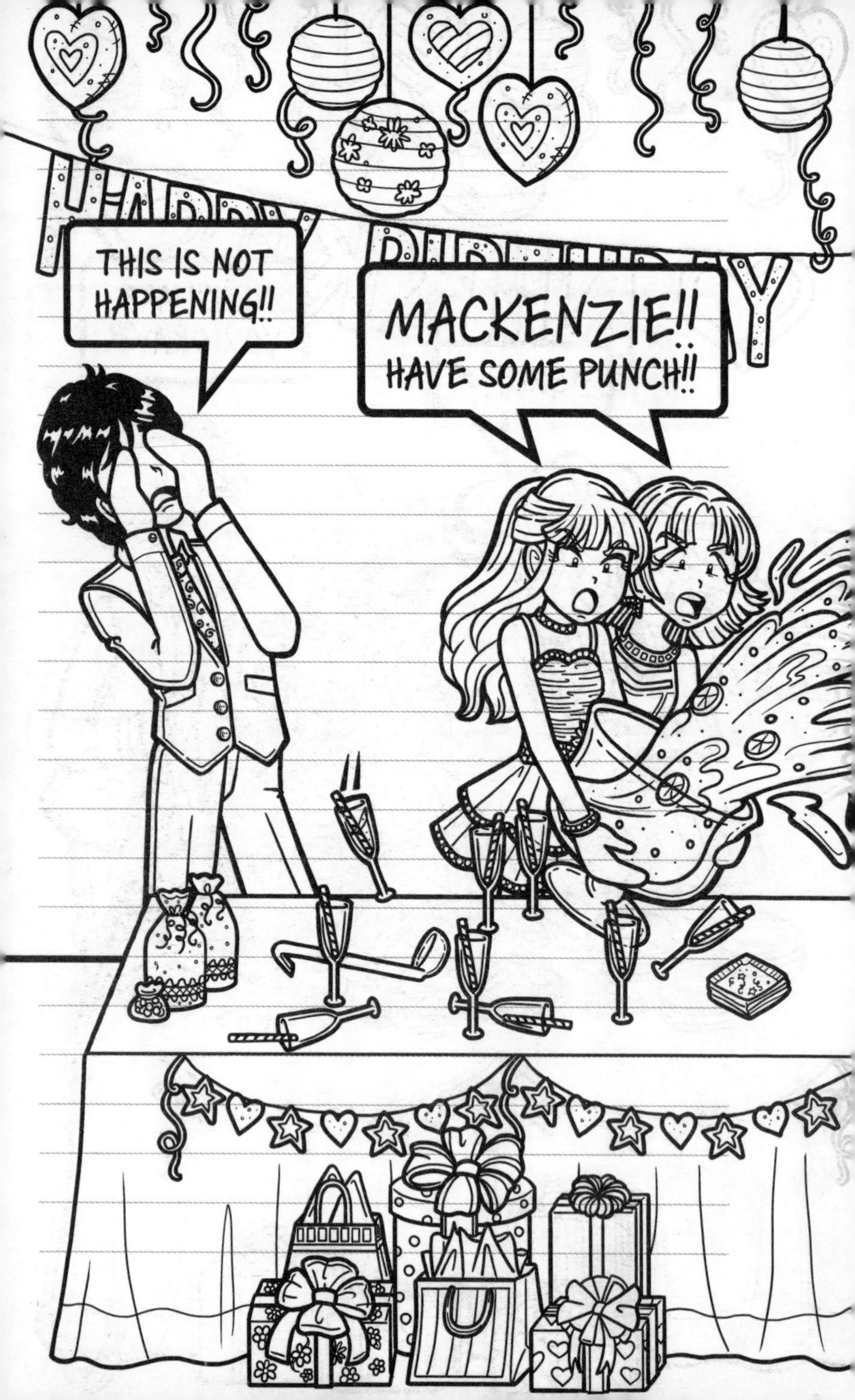
THIS IS NOT HAPPENING!!
MACKENZIE!! HAVE SOME PUNCH!!

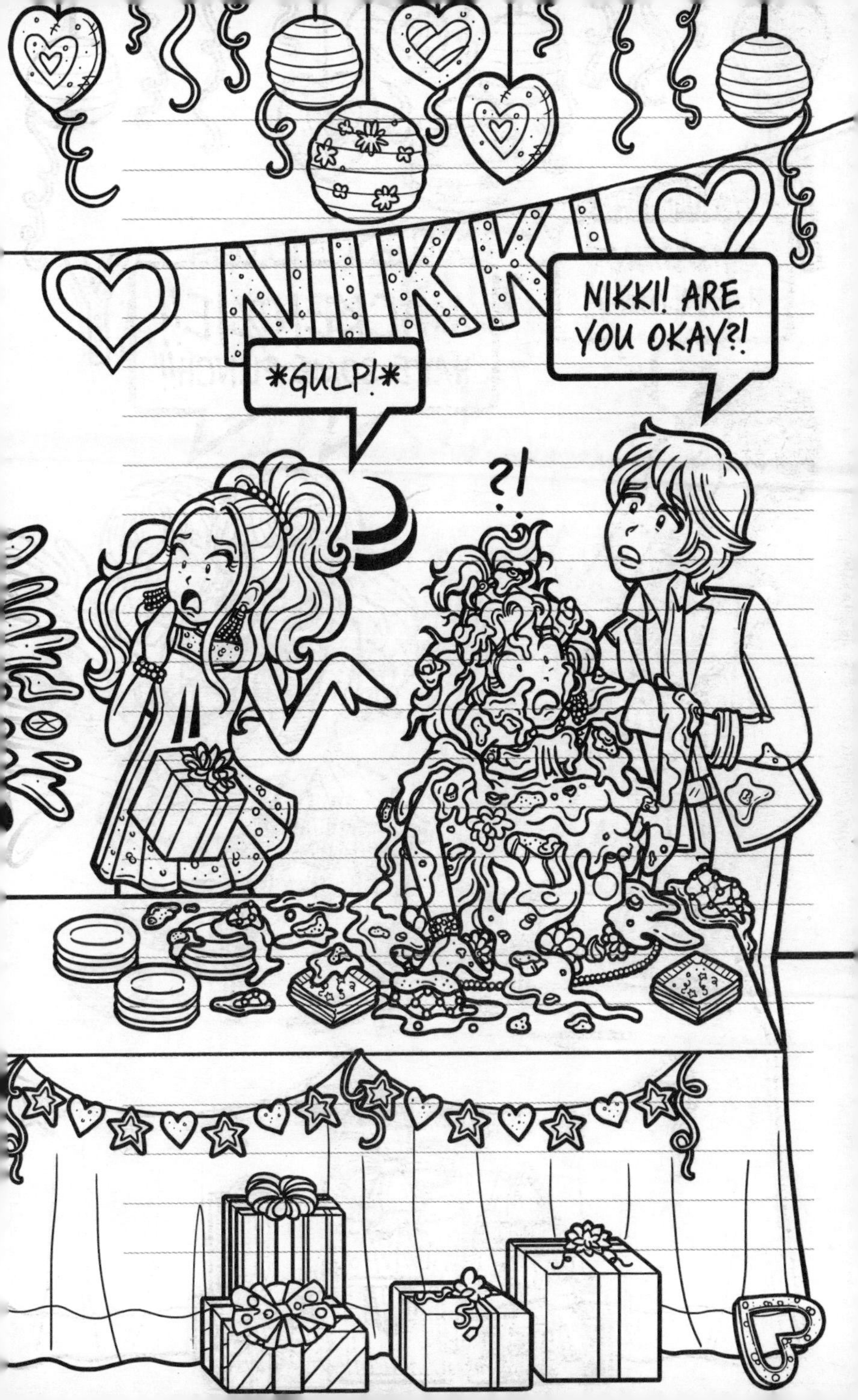
NIKKI
GULP!
NIKKI! ARE YOU OKAY?!
?!

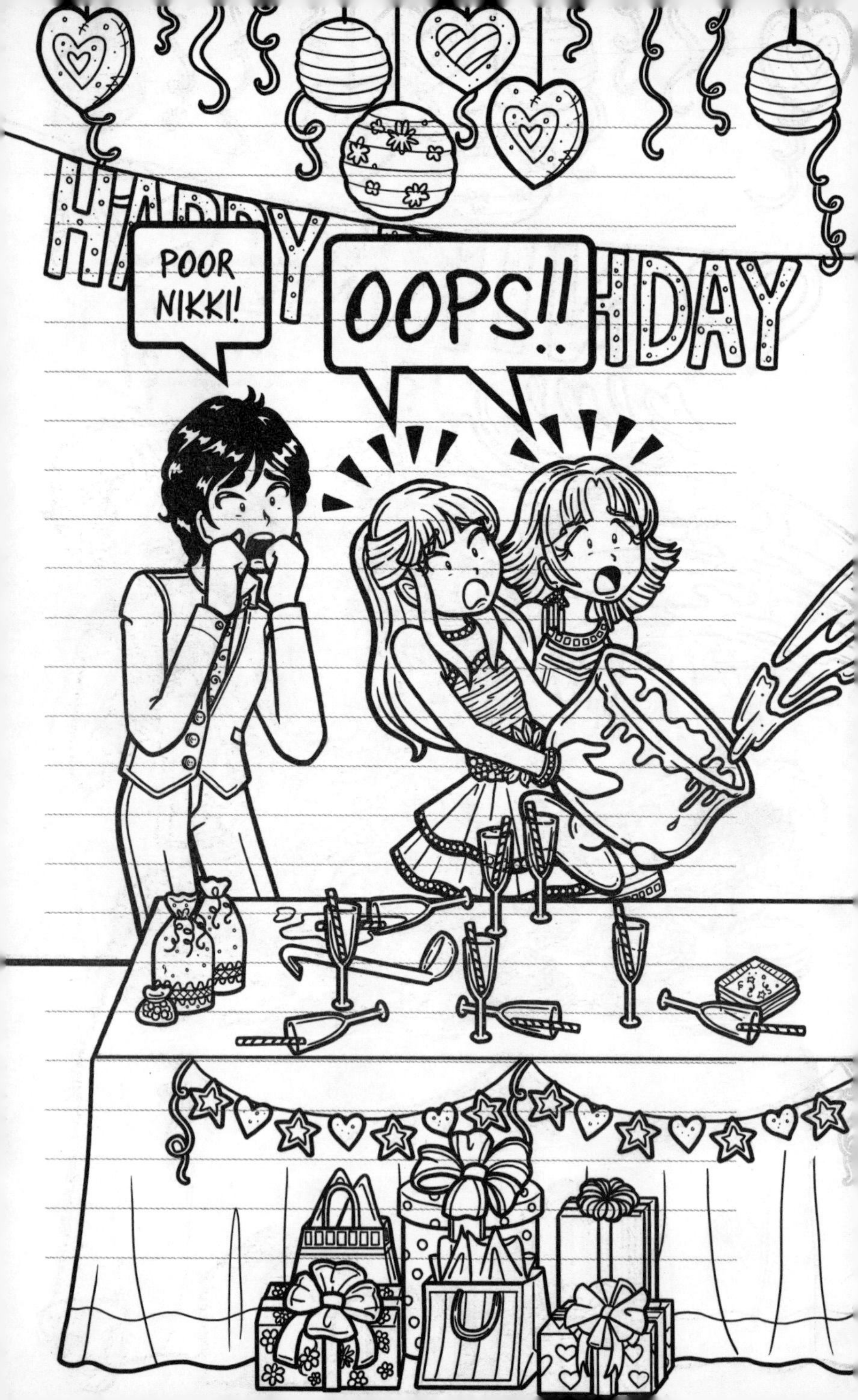
POOR NIKKI!
OOPS!!

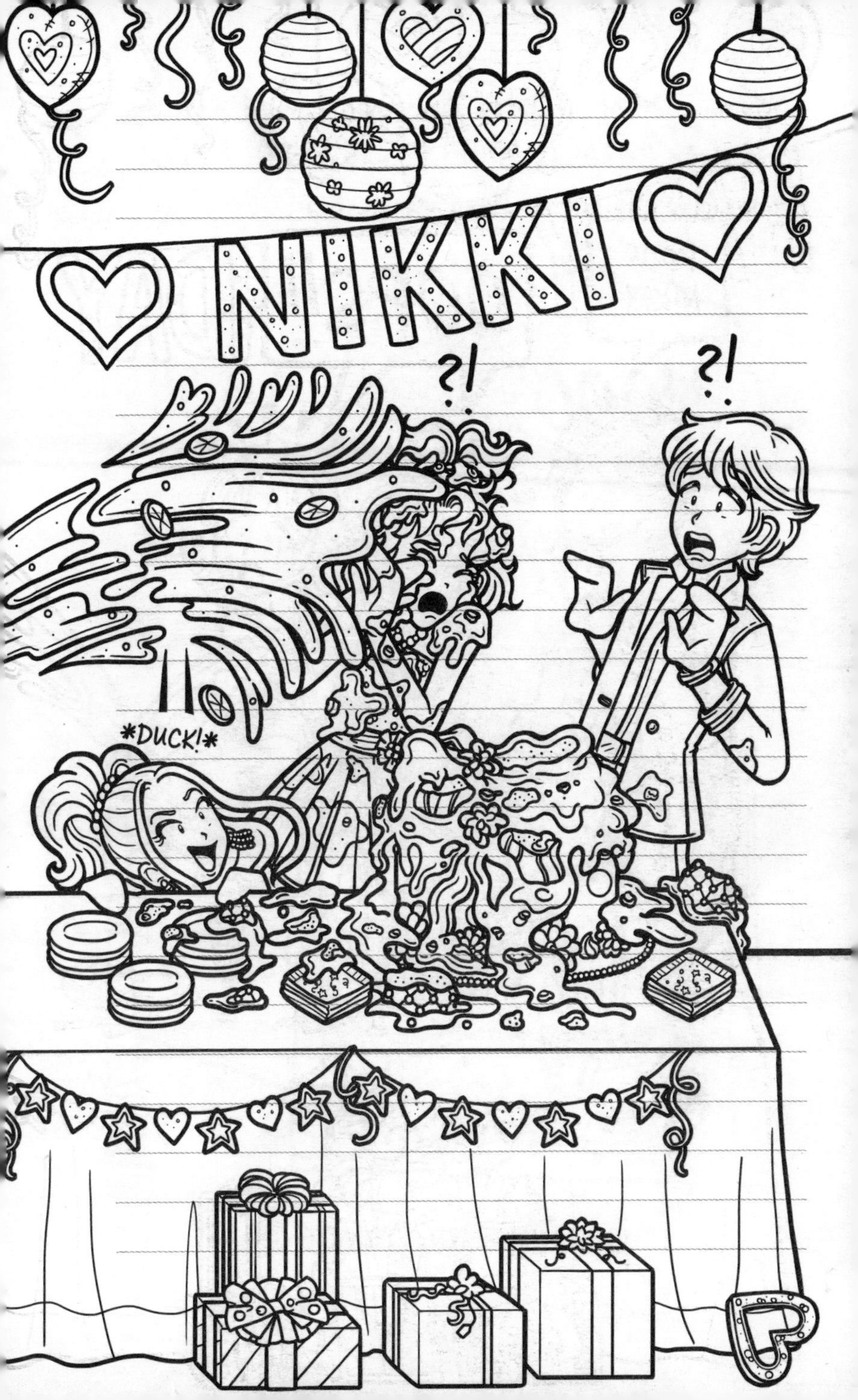
NIKKI
?!
?!
DUCK!

My wonderful birthday party had turned into a complete CATASTROPHE! It was AWFUL! Thank goodness the entire thing was just a . . .

HORRIBLE NIGHTMARE ☹!!

<u>OMG!</u> That dream felt SO real! I woke up FRANTIC in a cold sweat.

And now just the thought of having a party is totally FREAKING ME OUT.

I'm obviously suffering from a very serious and debilitating medical condition called CBPP, or CRUDDY BIRTHDAY PARTY PHOBIA.

It's an irrational fear of birthday party disasters.

I think I first contracted this illness on my fifth birthday. I had invited my ENTIRE kindergarten class to my party, and my dad dressed up as a clown.

He was HILARIOUS!

Until he was lighting the candles on my birthday cake and somehow accidentally set the seat of his baggy clown pants on fire.

Don't ask me HOW!

At first Dad panicked and ran around the room shouting, "FIRE! FIRE!"

Then he quickly put it out by SITTING in a huge bowl of fruit punch! . . .

SPLASH!

MY DAD, THE CLOWN, GETTING PUNCH!

All the kids laughed and cheered because they thought it was all part of his very funny clown act. But I was SO upset, I couldn't eat any of my birthday cake.

To this day, I have an extreme FEAR of clowns. Luckily, not ALL of them. Just SCREAMING CLOWNS with their BUTTS on FIRE!

I'm VERY serious! They practically scare the SNOT out of me.

DON'T LAUGH! It's NOT funny ☹!

Okay, maybe it IS kind of funny ☺.

But STILL!

Anyway, my birthday is on Saturday, June 28, and my BFFs, Chloe and Zoey, are BEGGING me to throw a big birthday party.

They're so excited about it that they're coming over tomorrow to help me plan everything.

Unfortunately, Chloe and Zoey are going to be SUPERdisappointed when I break the bad news that I've changed my mind. That scary dream has me worried that if even the TINIEST thing goes wrong, my birthday could turn into a complete DISASTER.

Hey, I'd LOVE to be the pretty and popular PARTY PRINCESS.

But come on! WHO am I kidding?!

MY life is NOT a fairy tale.

And I am NOT Cinderella.

Sorry! But if I dramatically dashed out of the royal ball at midnight in a glamorous, enchanted gown and lost my beautiful glass slipper, I'd step right in a pile of DOG POOP!

THURSDAY, JUNE 5

I'm STILL freaked out about my nightmare, and it keeps replaying in my head like a bad movie. I was covered from head to toe in so much frosting, I felt like a HUMAN cupcake ☹!

So today I planned to break the news to Chloe and Zoey that I've decided NOT to have a birthday party.

With all the things that could go WRONG, it was just not worth the risk. I hoped my BFFs would understand and be supportive.

They arrived at my house all fired up, with a HUGE stack of books and magazines about PARTY PLANNING. Just great ☹!

But I was totally shocked when they yelled, "SURPRISE!" and handed me a copy of a brand-new bestselling book.

I could NOT believe my eyes and just stared at it in AWE! . . .

It was a PARTY PLANNING book based on my
FAVE reality TV show, *My Very Rich and Trashy
Life!* Chloe and Zoey said it was an early birthday
present that I could use to plan my party.

And get this! They'd also ordered a large QUEASY
CHEESY pizza (which was a good thing, because all
that intense WORRYING about my party had made
me REALLY HUNGRY)!

It was quite obvious my BFFs were taking their
party planning duties VERY seriously ☹!

We ran upstairs and crashed in my bedroom. . . .

CHLOE, ZOEY, AND ME, PIGGING OUT
ON PIZZA WHILE READING BOOKS AND
MAGAZINES ABOUT PARTY PLANNING!

Although I appreciated their efforts, I finally gathered the courage to tell them the bad news. "Listen, guys, I'm really thankful you're helping me plan a big birthday bash. But, to be honest, I'd be perfectly happy with just the three of us hanging out in my backyard, trying not to choke on my dad's burnt hamburgers," I joked.

"Nikki, that's a GREAT idea!" Zoey exclaimed. "Look at this! The *My Very Rich and Trashy Life! Party Planner* has instructions for a FUN outdoor cookout." She showed me a page in the book. . . .

THROW A FAB OUTDOOR PARTY FOR FIFTY FRIENDS!

"It even suggests a midnight bonfire!" Chloe said. "OMG! That's going be SO ROMANTIC, right?! For YOU KNOW WHO . . . !" Then she started making silly kissing noises.

I kind of wanted to SLAP her. But I didn't. "That sounds really, um . . . interesting. But why don't the THREE of us just have a sleepover and watch some movies instead?" I insisted.

Chloe flipped through my new book. "Guess what?! Sleepovers are in here too. Look. . . ."

WATCH FUN FILMS WITH SEVENTY-FIVE FRIENDS!

"Now, THAT sounds really COOL!" Zoey giggled.

Okay. I was starting to get annoyed. "CHLOE! ZOEY! PLEASE! I really NEED you both to LISTEN!" I yelled. They got really quiet and just stared at me.

"Nikki, it's up to you! It's YOUR birthday. If you want a LISTENING party, that's fine with us." Chloe shrugged.

"I LOVE that idea!" Zoey exclaimed. She flashed us another page from the book. . . .

MUSIC LOVERS' LISTENING PARTY

INVITE ONE HUNDRED MUSIC LOVERS AND SHARE YOUR TOP TUNES!

"A listening party would actually be very RETRO and CHIC!" she said excitedly.

I could NOT believe my friends were so CLUELESS! That's when I totally lost it!

"COME ON, guys! I'm so EXASPERATED right now, I could just . . . SCREEEEAM!!" I ranted.

"Your book is AMAZING!" Chloe exclaimed. "There's actually a PARTY for THAT, too!!" . . .

Scream fest

A ROCK-'N'-RANT PARTY FOR TWO HUNDRED FUNKY FRIENDS!

"You could have a scream fest dance party for two hundred people in a warehouse!" Zoey suggested.

OMG! I felt like having a SCREAM FEST right there in my bedroom.

"PLEASE, JUST STOP! I don't want ANY of these parties! My life is SUPERstressful right now. It feels like I'm being tossed into the deep end of the popularity pool and I have to sink or swim. I know I'm supposed to just dive in, but I'm scared to death I might DROWN! Do you guys understand what I'm trying to say?"

Chloe and Zoey stared at each other and then at me as they nodded slowly.

"I hope you aren't MAD at me," I muttered.

"Nikki, WHY would we be mad at you?!" Zoey asked. "It's OUR fault that we didn't understand what you really wanted. We weren't listening."

"Now we HEAR you loud and clear!" Chloe said. "And it's perfectly fine with us if you want a . . ."

MY BFFS THINK I WANT A POOL PARTY?!

"A pool party is OUR first choice too!" Zoey shrieked in excitement.

"But we wanted to leave it totally up to YOU since it's YOUR birthday!" Chloe squealed.

"Luckily, your new book has an entire chapter on pool parties!" Zoey added.

Then my two BFFs started dancing around the room shouting, "POOL PAR-TAY! POOL PAR-TAY! NIKKI'S HAVING A POOL PAR-TAY!"

It was suddenly very clear that my BFFs wanted this birthday party REALLY, REALLY badly!

And as much as I was freaked out about the whole idea, I just didn't have the heart to disappoint them. So I jumped up and started dancing around the room with them and shouting, "POOL PAR-TAY! POOL PAR-TAY! I'M having a POOL PAR-TAY!"

Then we did a group hug! That's when Chloe and Zoey said the kindest, most sweetest thing anyone had EVER said to me.

"We're SO happy you're having this party, Nikki! You deserve it! And since you might be in Paris this summer, we really want to spend this special day just celebrating YOU!" Chloe explained.

26

"For once WE'LL get to do something NICE for you, to repay you for ALL the WONDERFUL things YOU'VE done for US!" Zoey exclaimed.

"Nikki! You're the GREATEST friend EVER!" they both gushed, and started to tear up.

OMG! Right then I felt VERY special! It's quite obvious that Chloe and Zoey truly CARE about me!

They're the BEST. FRIENDS. EVER!

And if having this birthday party will make THEM happy, then it will make ME happy too!

☺!!

PS: I should also be HAPPY that I WON'T have to see MacKenzie very much this summer. For once, my life will be DRAMA FREE!! WOO-HOO ☺!

School has been out for the summer for ONLY three days, and my BRATTY little sister, Brianna, is ALREADY driving me . . .

KA-RAY-ZEE ☹!

Ever since she earned her cooking badge in Scouts a few weeks ago, she's been obsessed with making nasty-tasting food unfit for human consumption.

You'd think that with practice, Brianna wouldn't be such an AWFUL cook.

I don't understand how it's possible, but instead of her cooking skills getting better, they seem to be getting worse!

When I came downstairs, Brianna was busy BURNING breakfast.

"Good morning! Are you hungry?" she asked.

"OMG!" I gagged as I plugged my nose. "Brianna, WHAT is that SMELL?!"

BRIANNA, COOKING UP YET ANOTHER
REALLY NASTY MEAL

Actually, it smelled HORRIBLE! Like ten-day-old garbage. Rotting in slimy swamp water.

Suddenly I noticed putrid black smoke pouring out of the toaster.

Brianna fanned the smoke and smiled.

"I'm cooking peanut-butter-covered SARDINES, swimming in ketchup and topped with gummy worms, all on toasted bread. It's a gourmet breakfast sandwich that I made up all by myself!" She beamed proudly.

"Brianna, that just sounds . . . UGH! I don't even have words to describe it!" I muttered.

Then I threw up in my mouth a little.

"How about DELISH?! It should be ready any second now . . . !" Brianna said as she stared at the toaster.

That's when I heard an earsplitting . . .

POP!

All I saw was a BLUR as Brianna's peanut butter, sardine, ketchup, and gummy worm sandwich shot out of that toaster like a ROCKET!

It hit the kitchen ceiling at eighty miles per hour with a loud . . .

SMACK!

. . . and stuck up there like glue. Melted gummy worm goo and ketchup dripped from the ceiling, making a rainbow-colored puddle on the floor.

"OOPS!" Brianna muttered, and then smirked like the huge mess on the ceiling and floor wasn't HER problem.

I was SO disgusted!!

"Brianna! Look at the MESS you just made. Your sardine sandwich is plastered up there like ceiling tiles. So WHAT are you going to do NOW?!"

Brianna giggled nervously. "Um, eat a big bowl of my marshmallow-spaghetti-'n'-meatball-popcorn cereal with milk instead?" She shrugged.

I gagged and threw up in my mouth AGAIN!

31

However, the HUMONGOUS MESS she left in the kitchen sink was even NASTIER than the sandwich stuck on the ceiling! . . .

BRIANNA LEAVES A PILE OF FIFTY-THREE
DIRTY DISHES IN THE KITCHEN SINK

"Sorry, Brianna! But I refuse to waste any more of my time and energy cleaning up your cooking DISASTERS," I fumed.

I decided to take matters into my own hands.

When Mom got home from work, I convinced her to get Brianna a toy she's been wanting FOREVER— the Princess Sugar Plum Lil' Chef Gourmet Cooking Set.

Not only would it be safer and easier for her to use, but it would ALSO keep her from TRASHING the kitchen, BURNING DOWN the house, and SHOOTING PROJECTILES out of the toaster.

I'm going to be SUPERbusy over the next few weeks planning my big birthday party.

And the LAST thing I need is to be distracted by Brianna cooking her nasty-tasting, foul-smelling, so-called FOOD!

Once all the Brianna drama was over, I decided to chillax with my puppy, Daisy, and work on the guest list for my party.

I was pleasantly surprised when I received a call on my cell phone from my crush, Brandon! . . .

I WAS HAPPY THAT BRANDON
ACTUALLY CALLED ME ☺!

He thanked me again for helping him with the Fuzzy Friends Animal Rescue Center charity drive. He was really happy because so far it had been a HUGE success.

And get this! Everyone LOVED the puppy artwork that I'd drawn for the website.

So Brandon came up with the brilliant idea to auction off my drawings to raise even MORE money! . . .

MY CUTE PUPPY DRAWINGS!

Then he asked me the question I'd been DREADING. . . .

"Nikki, I'm not trying to pressure you or anything! But have you made up your mind about whether you're going on that scholarship trip to Paris or on tour with our band, opening for the Bad Boyz this summer? We really need to start practice sessions with or without you so that we're prepared."

To be honest, I didn't have the slightest idea what I was going to do.

Just thinking about it gave me a massive headache and sweaty palms.

"You're right, Brandon. We really need to start band practice. But I'm STILL not sure what I plan to do this summer. I'll let you know as soon as I make a final decision."

"Okay, I understand. Listen, just so you'll have one LESS thing to worry about, the guys and I can start band practice tomorrow and just work on the music for the next few weeks. That will give you more time to figure things out," Brandon replied.

"What a GREAT idea! Then the vocals and choreography can just be added later on. Brandon, you're a LIFESAVER!" I gushed.

"No prob!" he said. "It sounds like you're going to have a busy summer. If there's anything I can do to help out, just let me know. Regardless of your final decision, I've got your back!"

"Thanks, Brandon! Actually, my summer is about to get even CRAZIER! I decided to have a birthday party this year, and Chloe and Zoey are helping plan it. It's going to be on Saturday, June 28! You're definitely invited!"

"Wow! You're having a party, too?! So when do you plan to get any SLEEP?!" Brandon teased. "Thank you for the invite! I'm really looking forward to it."

"I am too!" I giggled.

That's when things suddenly got kind of AWKWARD. We didn't have anything to say, but we didn't want to hang up. Finally he said . . .

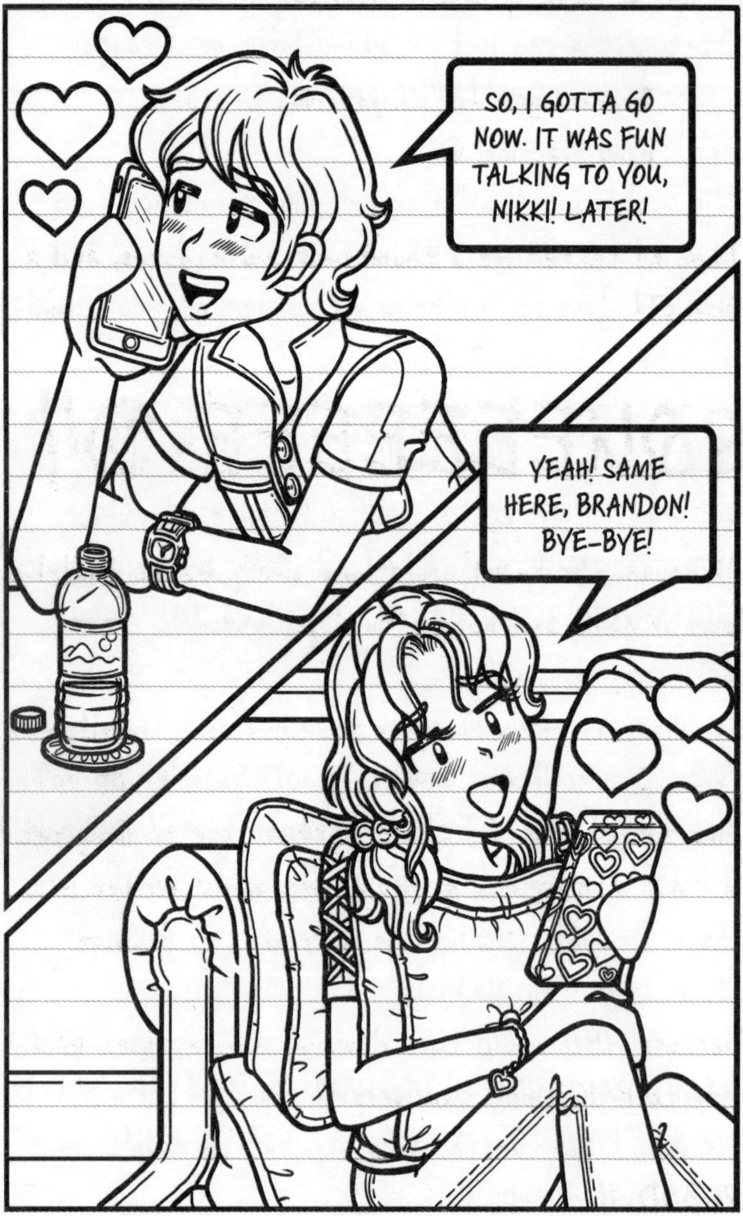
SO, I GOTTA GO NOW. IT WAS FUN TALKING TO YOU, NIKKI! LATER!
YEAH! SAME HERE, BRANDON! BYE-BYE!

After we hung up, I sent Brandon a text. . . .

> Thanks again for volunteering to start
> band practice! ☺

Then he texted me a thumbs—up, music notes, and a
HEART!

SQUEEEEEEE ☺!!

Although, the heart could have simply meant that he
loves MUSIC and not . . . um, you know!

I realize I'm really lucky to have him as a friend.

And even if I DITCH the Bad Boyz tour to hang out
in Paris with my new friend André, whose father lives
there, Brandon said he'll be okay with my decision.

Because WHO would turn down an all-expenses-paid
trip to PARIS for two weeks?!

NOBODY!!

So I have NOTHING at all to worry about, RIGHT?!

WRONG!!

WHO am I kidding?!

I REALLY, REALLY like Brandon.

A LOT!!

So I need to be VERY careful, or I could end up DESTROYING our friendship.

FOREVER!!

☹!!

SATURDAY, JUNE 7

NOTE TO SELF: The next time Mom says, "Hey, Nikki, let's have some quality GIRL TIME with just YOU and ME," suggest a movie.

Or frozen yogurt. Or getting our nose hairs PAINFULLY plucked out one at a time.

But NOT a mother-daughter YOGA CLASS ☹!!

I mean, I have nothing against yoga. I'm sure it's great for some people. Maybe I'll even enjoy it MYSELF one day.

But TODAY was NOT that day!

Mom wanted to unwind from an unusually stressful week at work and had a two-for-one coupon for this new yoga studio in our neighborhood.

I didn't have anything better to do. And since I almost NEVER get time with just my mom, I said yes.

BIG MISTAKE 🙁!!

I knew it the moment we walked into that place.

All the women wore fancy exercise clothes that matched their yoga mats. They just stared at us and whispered to each other. Probably because Mom was wearing a ripped, tie-dyed T-shirt and faded gym shorts from her college days.

It was quite obvious these ladies didn't want us in their class. I got a huge knot in my stomach when I realized they were just like the CCPs (Cute, Cool & Popular kids) at my middle school. But all GROWN UP!

Mom's eyes glazed over as she swayed to the weird new age music and inhaled the lavender-sage incense. I totally ignored my primal urge to run out of there SCREAMING.

Everyone in the class had their own fancy yoga mats in fancy yoga bags, but we pulled two from a pile in the corner.

Yep! DUSTY, GERMY mats covered in other people's SWEAT that smelled like dirty gym socks stuffed with pickle relish.

JUST GREAT ☹!

I was expecting the instructor to be a slender young lady in her twenties, but I was WAY off. She was older than my mom, with a SUPERathletic body and her long gray hair in a braid.

Mom eagerly unrolled her mat at the front of the room, right next to the instructor.

"Mom!" I whisper-shouted. "Since we're new, I think we should probably be in the back."

But what I really meant was, "Mom! Do we really want to publicly HUMILIATE ourselves by being front and center so EVERYONE can LAUGH at us?!"

"Actually, Nikki, we're beginners, so the closer we are to the instructor, the better!" Mom said cheerfully as she waved hello to everyone.

MOM, PICKING A REALLY BAD SPOT!

44

"Your mom is right." The instructor smiled. "Just do what you can and always remember to breathe," she said calmly.

I snorted and then turned it into a cough.

BREATHE?! Did she ACTUALLY think I would FORGET to breathe? WHO does that?!!

My thoughts were rudely interrupted when two students entered the room.

"Hello, ladies!" our instructor chirped. "Why don't you set up over here by our newcomers?" She explained proudly to Mom and me, "They're my STAR students! Just keep an eye on them, and you'll learn the perfect technique."

OMG! You'd never guess who's a SUPERadvanced yoga student!

MACKENZIE HOLLISTER, that's who ☹!!

And, apparently, her mom.

45

They sashayed over together with matching mats, towels, water bottles, and duffel bags. I was pretty sure MacKenzie's yoga pants cost more than my mom's CAR! I am so NOT lying.

MacKenzie wrinkled up her nose at me like my yoga mat was old, dirty, and smelled really bad.

Well, okay. All of that was TRUE.

But STILL!

MacKenzie is such a BIG FAKE! She gave me a phony smile and placed her mat near mine. For some reason, she pretended to be nice—probably because her guru was watching.

"Okay, everyone! Let's warm up," the teacher said.

I had barely managed to bend over when MacKenzie immediately began to pose her body into shapes NO HUMAN BODY was meant to make!

I hated to admit it, but she was AMAZING! ...

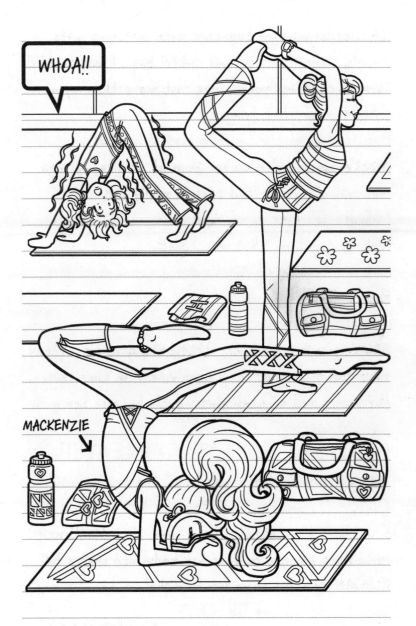

MACKENZIE IS AWESOME AT YOGA!

Her mother was pretty good too!

"Very nice, MacKenzie!" our teacher said.

But as soon as the teacher turned her back,
MacKenzie rolled her eyes at me.

I almost fell over on my mat.

But not because of MacKenzie. I got a huge, very
painful CRAMP in my leg!

Now, remember what the teacher said about not
forgetting to breathe? I'd only been in the class
for about ten minutes when . . .

I TOTALLY FORGOT TO BREATHE ☹!

OMG! Do you have any idea how HARD yoga is?!!

FIRST of all, this was some kind of torture yoga
where they make the room really warm like a sauna.
Soon I was sweating BUCKETS.

That seemed DANGEROUS! I could slip in a puddle of my OWN sweat and rupture my spleen.

SECOND of all, I thought yoga was sitting cross-legged, quietly meditating while humming the word "OMMMMM" like they do on TV.

Sorry, but it's NOT!

So don't believe the hype.

I was screaming, "OW! That HURTS!" in my head while I tried to do all the weird, uncomfortable poses.

Within minutes I was in so much pain, I thought I was going to DIE!

My mom was struggling too. But she had that fierce, determined look on her face like she was NOT going to give up.

So I decided NOT to give up either!

ESPECIALLY in front of MacKenzie!

UNTIL . . .

I had a little "situation" during yoga class.

OMG! I thought I was going to DIE! Not from pain, but EMBARRASSMENT.

I really don't want to stop writing in the middle of this diary entry, but my mom just called me down for dinner.

I'll try to finish this tomorrow.

I just hope we're NOT having leftovers. AGAIN!

☹!

Okay! I can FINALLY finish the diary entry from yesterday. . . .

So, I was in that yoga class, pretty much dying of embarrassment! WHY?!

My yoga teacher gave us a minute to rest in this position called "child's pose."

It basically involves curling up in a little ball and silently crying into your yoga mat, begging for the TORTURE to end!

NOT! I'll admit I made that last part up about crying into your mat.

Anyway, this was the first pose that actually felt comfortable. I even relaxed! But do you have any idea what happens when you relax in that position?!

Child's pose should come with a WARNING!

I accidentally let out an enormously LOUD and LONG, um . . . well, I'll just put it this way. . . .

It kind of sounded like a four-thousand-pound hippopotamus BURPING. . . .

HIPPO

Only, mine WASN'T a burp, because it came out of the other end.

And if THAT weren't bad enough, it happened while the room was completely quiet.

I totally FREAKED OUT! And my mom did too. . . .

ME, HAVING A **SUPER**EMBARRASSING
MOMENT IN YOGA CLASS

OMG! Even MacKenzie couldn't keep up her phony ZEN YOGI act after that. She actually looked shocked, angry, and nauseated. All at the same time!

I cringed as my face turned bright red. . . .

ME, SO HUMILIATED,
I WANTED TO DIG A DEEP HOLE,
CRAWL INTO IT, AND DIE!

54

The teacher gazed at me sympathetically. "It's all right, dear," she said loudly. "In fact, it's a good thing. Passing wind just indicates you're relaxing important muscles."

OMG! I couldn't take it anymore! I mumbled an excuse about needing to use the restroom and rushed out of the class.

"Congratulations!" the teacher yelled after me. "Your BOWELS are happy and healthy!"

The LAST thing I wanted or needed was for the teacher to discuss the condition of my bowels! Especially in front of MacKenzie Hollister!!

Mom came out a minute later, her face still flushed and covered with sweat.

"I'm sorry, Mom," I muttered. "You can finish the class if you want. I'll just wait out here."

Mom gave me a weak smile as we watched the front desk lady light more incense.

I couldn't help but wonder if it was to get rid of the smell of my, um . . . stinky situation!

"I think we've both had enough yoga for today," Mom said, squeezing my hand. "Come on. Let's go!"

We walked out of the dim studio into the bright sunshine and gulped the fresh air.

Mom checked the time on her cell phone. "We've still got a half hour before we have to pick Brianna up from her ballet class. So why don't we grab a scoop of ice cream?"

The ice-cream shop next door to the yoga studio is definitely MY kind of place. No incense or snooty ladies judging me. And, best of all, no MacKenzie Hollister.

Just bright colors, loud pop music, and so many sugary sweet toppings, I get hyper just looking at them.

But I still couldn't shake the AWFUL feeling of what had just happened back at the yoga studio.

I mean, it would have been BAD enough in a room full of strangers. But in front of MACKENZIE?! I could just imagine all the nasty things she was going to post on social media. Very soon EVERYONE at my school was going to be GOSSIPING about me and LAUGHING at me!

OMG! What if my CRUSH, Brandon, sees it ☹?!

Before I knew it, big, fat tears were rolling down my cheeks. . . .

"Oh, sweetheart!" My mom sighed as she pulled me close and gave me a big hug. "I think this calls for a super-deluxe hot fudge sundae with extra whipped cream."

She ordered, and I tried to stop being so upset.

I just HATE when MacKenzie makes me feel like that!

"Did I ever tell you about the time I threw up on my prom date?" my mom asked, obviously trying to change the subject as we walked to a table.

"MOM!! NO WAY!" I gasped.

She explained how she'd eaten some bad shrimp at the fancy restaurant before prom and then vomited all over her date during their first slow dance.

"You actually THREW UP on your PROM date?!" I giggled. "Did you transfer to a new school after that? Wait! I bet your prom date transferred to a new school after that! I would have!"

I have to admit, HER horror story made me feel a little better about MINE.

"So, did that guy ever speak to you again?!"

Her eyes twinkled, and she tried to hide a smile.

"Spill it, Mom! That guy NEVER, EVER spoke to you again, right?!"

"Actually, we speak all the time," she said smugly.

"NO WAY!" I sputtered. "Really?"

Her phone buzzed, and she glanced at it. "In fact, that's HIM texting me right now!"

I could not believe my mom was actually BLUSHING!!

Okay, NOW I was dying of curiosity.

I quickly leaned forward to sneak a peek at her phone and was a little shocked to see . . .

MY DAD'S FACE!

"DAD?! The prom guy was DAD?!"
I shrieked. "Why haven't you ever told me this
story before?!"

My mom grinned at me.

"Of course, it felt like a HUGE deal back then, Nikki.
But now it's just one more thing in life that didn't
quite go as planned. What's a little vomit on our
first date when we've been through two childbirths,
plus opening a business and moving to a new city, all
while raising two beautiful daughters? Hey, that prom
dinner disaster was NOTHING when you live with a
sweet little Princess Sugar Plum—addicted hurricane
in pigtails like . . ."

Mom and I exchanged knowing glances as we both
blurted out . . .

"BRIANNA!"

I started to giggle.

Then Mom started to laugh.

Soon we were both SNORTING into our hot fudge
sundae! . . .

MOM AND ME, TALKING ABOUT LIFE
AS WE SHARE A HOT FUDGE SUNDAE!

That hot fudge sundae was DELISH!

I have to admit, it was fun hanging out with my mom today.

She's actually kind of COOL!

In spite of being a MOM and wearing that very TACKY outfit from her college days.

Now, THIS is the kind of quality GIRL TIME I could get used to!

☺!

Since it was a perfect summer day, Chloe, Zoey, and I decided to meet up at the park to continue planning my party. I brought Daisy along too.

"Nikki, your pool party is going to be EPIC!" Chloe exclaimed.

"It'll be SO epic that kids will STILL be TALKING about it on the FIRST day of school!" Zoey raved.

"And because of YOUR very cool party, everyone will be DYING to invite US to THEIR parties!" Chloe explained.

"Nikki and Chloe, do you realize this could change our lives?!" Zoey said wistfully. "We could become the most POPULAR kids at school!"

WOW! All this party stuff was making me feel light-headed. Or maybe Daisy's leash was cutting off the blood circulation to my brain. . . .

MY BFFS AND ME, EXCITEDLY PLANNING MY
PARTY WHILE DAISY MAKES A FRIEND!

The fact that my birthday party might impact our social status at school next year made me a little nervous. What if something goes wrong?!

But my BFFs assured me that everything was going to be just fine!

"Don't worry, Nikki!" Chloe said. "Since I know EVERYTHING about parties, I'll be your social director. I've had three parties for my brother, and everyone is still talking about the last one."

"I know, Chloe. But everyone is STILL talking about it because of that little problem you had with your game, remember?" I reminded her.

Chloe rolled her eyes at me and folded her arms. "Hey, it wasn't MY fault I had to call 911 during that game of Simon Says because my little brother stuck a cheesy snack up his nose. And THEN all the other kids stuck cheesy snacks up THEIR noses because Simon said to. Nikki, I could have totally lost it and FREAKED OUT! But I didn't. I was calm and handled my business!" . . .

CHLOE, CALLING 911 ABOUT
A CHEESY SNACK EMERGENCY!

I had to admit that Chloe had a really good point. I couldn't have handled ONE kid with a cheesy snack stuck up his nose, let alone SIX!

I would have totally lost it when all those emergency vehicles arrived with sirens blaring.

Chloe was practically a HERO! Well, kind of.

"Nikki, don't forget that I've attended some awesome celebrity sweet sixteen parties with my dad," Zoey explained. "So I'm pretty much a party EXPERT. I'll be your activities director."

"Thanks, Zoey! But weren't most of those parties SUPERexpensive?" I asked.

"That's true," Zoey admitted. "But instead of hiring the Bad Boyz to perform at your party, we could have a DJ. And instead of the sushi bar and the climbing wall, we could have Frappuccinos and a zip line. That would drastically reduce our budget by about 18%!" she explained as she crunched the numbers on her calculator.

WAIT! Did Zoey just say "ZIP LINE"?! What if I'm ALLERGIC to zip lines?! . . .

AAAH!!

ME, HAVING A SEVERE ALLERGIC
REACTION TO A ZIP LINE!

"Um, won't a zip line cost a lot?" I asked.

"Don't worry. If we're on a tight budget, we can always cut out more stuff," Zoey answered.

"Listen, guys, to be honest, I don't even HAVE a budget! Unless you count the $8.73 I have hidden in my sock drawer," I muttered. . . .

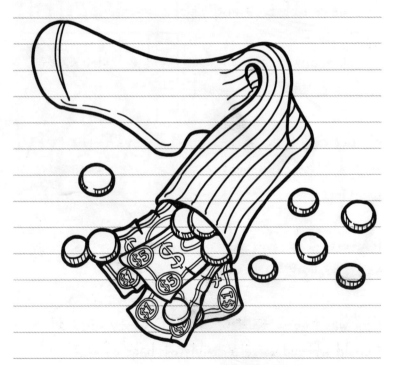

MY LIFE SAVINGS OF $8.73 THAT IS
HIDDEN IN MY SOCK DRAWER!

That's when Zoey kind of stared at me and blinked her eyes really fast.

"OMG! Our party budget is only $8.73?!" she muttered. "Well, okay! Let's not panic! We could use that for the, um . . . Frappuccinos, I think. Actually, that would only buy the ICE for the Frappuccinos. Like maybe two small bags of ice. But we're off to a really good start."

Thank goodness Zoey is an expert on celeb parties AND a FINANCIAL wizard!

We decided that an island luau party theme with a HUGE swimming pool would be fun and exciting.

However, in spite of my BFFs' enthusiasm, I suddenly had a really BAD feeling about my party.

How was I going to have an EPIC party when all I could afford were a couple of bags of ice?!

It was going to be a JOKE!

Unless I could come up with the cash to buy all the party stuff I needed.

I could do the responsible thing and get a job and try to earn the money myself. But that could take weeks, or even months.

Desperate times call for desperate measures.

So I'll just have to convince my parents to pay the extra money for a fancier island luau birthday party.

Unfortunately, having a child my age is VERY expensive.

But it's NOT my problem.

My parents should have thought of that BEFORE I was BORN!

☺!!

GREAT NEWS ☺! Chloe, Zoey, and I have finally figured out all the details for my island luau birthday party.

OMG! It's going to be AWESOME! However, we still have one small complication: the COST. Even though we got rid of the zip line and a few other things, it's more money than I have. Which, by the way, is still only $8.73 ☹!

But my BFFs told me not to worry about those minor details when my parents can pay for it.

Since we need water for an island party (DUH!), it was Zoey's idea (as my activities director) to have it at the brand-new community pool. The cost to rent it is $250, but the payment is not due until three days before the party.

We found the PERFECT party invitations at a fancy card shop in the mall. Zoey insisted on loaning me her babysitting money to buy them.

OMG! They're SUPERcute! . . .

MY BIRTHDAY PARTY INVITATIONS!

I was going to invite about twenty people. But Chloe (as my social director) suggested that I invite kids from North Hampton Hills International Academy and South Ridge Middle School, along with kids from our school, Westchester Country Day. So we ended up with a guest list of one hundred!

We had a BLAST hanging out at Chloe's house working on the invitations. . . .

CHLOE, ZOEY, AND ME,
WORKING ON MY BIRTHDAY INVITES!

Since my party was going to be FABULOUS, Chloe and Zoey thought it would be a good idea to invite some of the CCPs.

Of course, I wasn't too excited about that, mainly because of that nightmare I'd had.

But Chloe and Zoey made the very good point that if WE want to be invited to some of the best parties at school, we needed to invite a wide variety of classmates.

We also decided to invite my worst FRENEMY!

YES! MACKENZIE HOLLISTER!

But we weren't inviting her to be friendly.

We were pretty sure MY birthday party was going to be better than HER birthday party. And once MacKenzie figured this out, she'd go into a JEALOUS rage and have an extremely INTENSE and PAINFUL reaction right at my party in front of EVERYONE! . . .

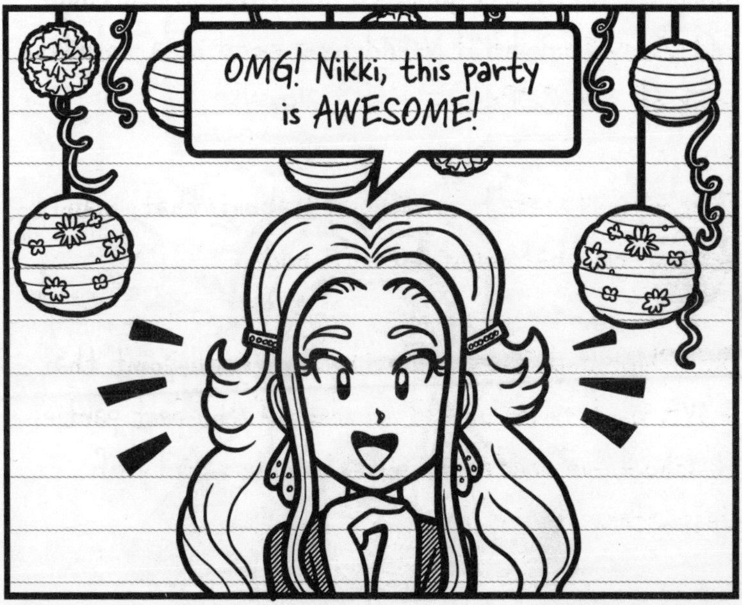
OMG! Nikki, this party is AWESOME!

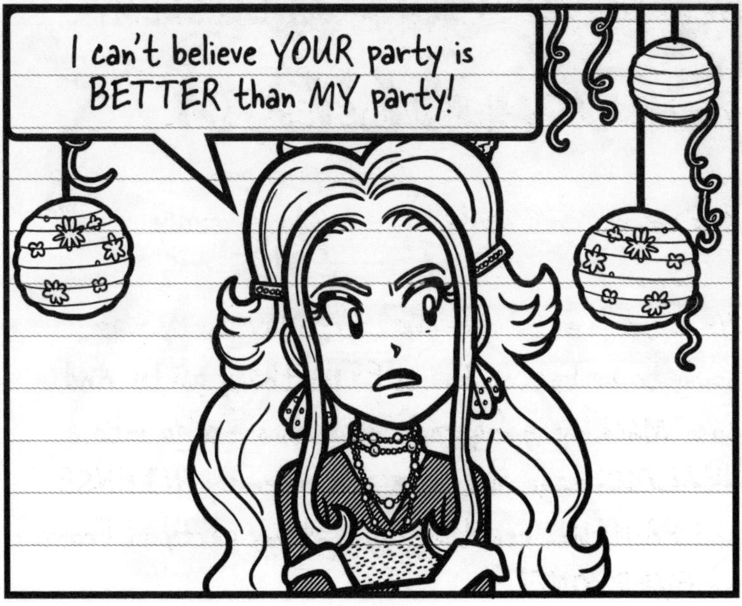
I can't believe YOUR party is BETTER than MY party!

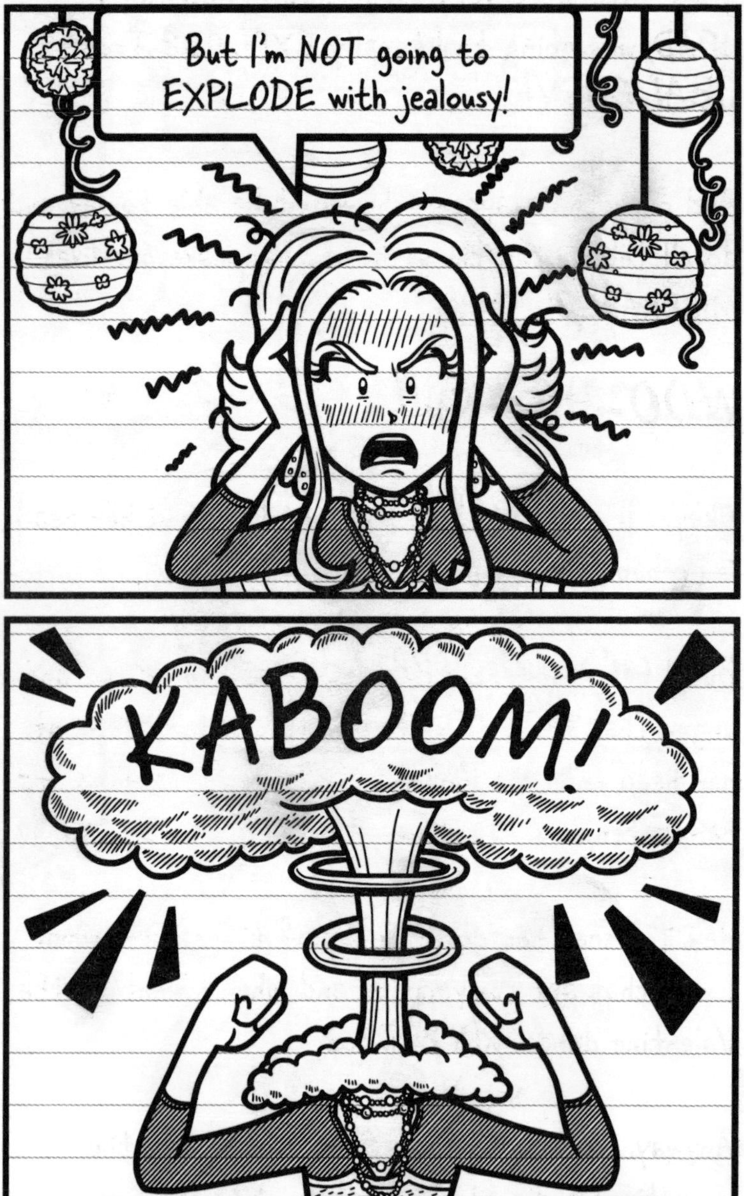
But I'm NOT going to EXPLODE with jealousy!
KABOOM!

YEP! We were very sure that MacKenzie's HEAD was going to literally EXPLODE from JEALOUSY!

And once that happens, she won't be able to say and do all those mean things to us that make our lives MISERABLE!

WOO-HOO ☺!!

Okay, I'll admit that I'm exaggerating, and her head is probably NOT going to explode.

But I bet MacKenzie IS going to get so jealous and angry that her EYES are going to BULGE out of her head until she looks like a TOAD in lip gloss and hair extensions.

Hey, I've seen her do it plenty of times. Like when I won that art competition and when I went to the Valentine dance with Brandon.

Anyway, we decided that Chloe would keep the invitations and mail them out on June 16.

I'm FINALLY starting to get SUPERexcited about my party, and now I'm actually looking forward to it!

It's going to be AWESOME!

Even though I initially had second thoughts about having a big birthday bash, I'm SO happy I decided to do it.

I'm really thankful for Chloe and Zoey and all their encouragement and hard work planning everything.

I couldn't have done it without them.

Now all we have left to do is order the birthday cake, arrange the music, and buy the party decorations!

Planning a big party for one hundred people has been fun, exciting, and A LOT easier than I thought it would be.

As soon as we finish up the last few items on our checklist, we'll be DONE with my party.

TWO weeks ahead of time!

SQUEEEE ☺!

I was FREAKING OUT for no reason at all.

We're SUPERorganized and in total control!

Hey! WHAT could go WRONG?!

!!

NOTE TO SELF: Ask Mom and Dad for a new bike for my birthday! Brianna rode my bike without permission and left it in the driveway BEHIND Dad's roach van. He ran over it, and now my frame is bent and the wheels make a loud squealing noise whenever I ride it ☹! I'd ALSO like a replacement sister for my birthday.

I was SO happy and excited about my party when I woke up this morning. It's almost all I ever think about.

I'm actually counting down the days on a calendar that I taped to the back of my bedroom door.

When I checked my cell, I was shocked to see that I had received twenty-seven calls, forty-nine e-mails, and fifty-four text messages!

And they were ALL about . . .

MY BIRTHDAY PARTY!!

Somehow, word had gotten out, and now EVERYONE was talking about it.

And it was not just the kids at WCD. Students at North Hampton Hills and South Ridge were buzzing about it too.

I didn't have the slightest idea how everyone had found out about my party, since we hadn't sent out the invitations yet.

Although it PROBABLY had something to do with the fact that my social director, Chloe, had posted my invitation on social media.

It had already gotten 357 likes!

And my activities director, Zoey, had posted a photo of the colorful flower garden at the community pool that looked like a real tropical island retreat!

It had already gotten 310 likes!

OMG!

People I didn't even know were BEGGING for an invitation to MY party!

I decided to have an emergency Skype meeting with Chloe and Zoey to discuss the situation. . . .

ME, TALKING TO CHLOE AND ZOEY
ONLINE ABOUT MY BIRTHDAY PARTY

I was a little nervous about all the attention that my party was getting. But Chloe and Zoey insisted that it was a good thing because it meant people were dying to attend. Chloe said that since she was my social director, I could forward all the messages I'd received to her and she would answer them for me.

Then my BFFs asked me if I wanted to increase my guest list from one hundred to one hundred and fifty people. Or maybe even to two hundred people!

I was like, "Thanks, guys! But SORRY! I don't think I even KNOW two hundred people!!"

However, our conversation was interrupted when Brandon called me on video chat on my cell phone.

SQUEEEEEEE ☺!

My BFFs and I agreed to end our conversation so I could talk to Brandon. Chloe and Zoey said they'd Skype me again in ten minutes so we could finish discussing my party.

"Hi, Brandon!" I said, smoothing my hair down. I was worried that it looked like I'd just stuck my thumb in an electrical socket.

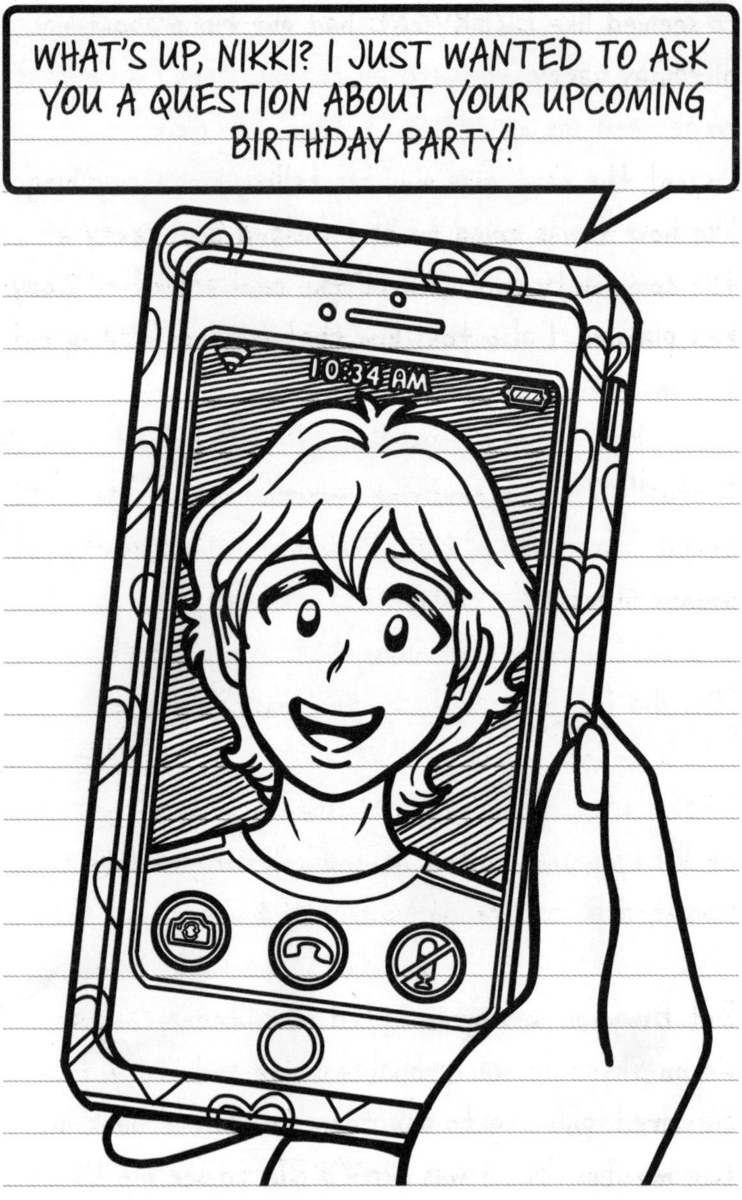
WHAT'S UP, NIKKI? I JUST WANTED TO ASK YOU A QUESTION ABOUT YOUR UPCOMING BIRTHDAY PARTY!
10:34 AM

It seemed like EVERYONE had questions about my birthday party.

I spent the next five minutes telling him everything, like how it was going to be an island luau party at the community pool, and all the cool activities Zoey had planned. I also told him that we'd be mailing out the invitations on June 16.

"Actually, I saw everything on social media." He smiled. "Everyone is talking about it. Your party sounds like fun!"

"So, did I answer all your questions?" I asked.

That's when he nervously brushed his bangs out of his eyes and kind of blushed. "Well, actually, I wanted to ask you if you'd like to—"

But Brandon was interrupted by someone calling me on Skype. It was probably Chloe and Zoey. I answered, planning to ask them to call me back in five minutes. But I was SHOCKED to see . . .

"OH, WOW!" I sputtered in surprise. "Hi, André!
How are you doing?"

OMG! I just sat there STUNNED! And a little . . . um, FREAKED OUT!

WHY?!

Because I was talking to BRANDON on my cell phone and ANDRÉ on my laptop.

AT EXACTLY THE SAME TIME ☹!!

I could BARELY manage to talk to EACH of them ALONE, let alone TOGETHER!

I was hoping that they couldn't see or hear each other. Then I'd just hang up on BOTH of them. And later I'd call each guy back, pretending that his call had dropped.

I thought it was an ingenious plan to get out of a very sticky situation. But, unfortunately, the guys COULD see and hear each other. JUST GREAT ☹!!

This is how their conversation went:

89

ANDRÉ: Brandon?! Is that you? I hope I'm not interrupting anything important. Although, considering everything, I highly doubt it.

BRANDON: Actually, André, as usual, YOU ARE! It would be really COOL if you'd go interrupt somewhere else.

ANDRÉ: My apologies, Brandon. I'll just call Nicole back later. You know, after she finishes your BABYSITTING session and your mum puts you down for your nap!

BRANDON: DUDE! Her name ISN'T Nicole, it's NIKKI! And BABYSITTING?! You really need to go get some breath spray. All that GARBAGE you're TALKING is starting to STINK so bad that I can smell it through the PHONE!

ANDRÉ: Actually, Brandon, that smell is probably your DIAPER!

ME: COME ON, GUYS! Can you at least PRETEND you're NOT three-year-old spoiled BRATS and TRY to get along?!

BRANDON: Hey, HE started it!

ANDRÉ: NO! HE started it, and I just finished it!

BRANDON: No, I didn't!

ANDRÉ: Yes, you did!

BRANDON: NO, I DIDN'T!

ANDRÉ: YES, YOU DID! Sorry, Nicole! I was just calling to ask you an important question about your party. It's all over social media.

BRANDON: Her name isn't NICOLE! Why do you keep calling her that? Anyway, NIKKI, before WE were so rudely interrupted by Mr. Diaper Breath, I was about to ask you a question.

ME: Listen, guys! You're BOTH invited to my party. Although, after all this, I'm seriously having second thoughts. I might just drop both of you off at Toddler Time DAY CARE! Anyway, WHAT did you each want to ASK me?! . . .

ME, TOTALLY CONFUSED WHEN BRANDON
AND ANDRÉ ASK ME THE SAME QUESTION!

So WHAT did I do?

I had a total MELTDOWN and PANICKED!
Then I started to LIE like a rug. . . .

"Listen, guys! Your connections are really BAD, and
I can barely hear a word you're saying! SHHHHHHHHHH!
Did you hear all that static? SHHHHHHH!! I really
need to go right now because SHHHHHHH!! Sorry, but
I think both your calls are about to drop. SHHHHHH!
So I'll call you both back later. BYE! SHHHH!"

CLICK! I disconnected Brandon on my cell.

CLICK! I disconnected André on my laptop.

Yes, I know! Faking static and dropped calls was
dishonest, immature, and pathetic!

But WHAT was I supposed to do when they were
fighting and put me on the spot like that?!

Although, to be honest, NEITHER of them
DESERVES to be my date at my birthday party.

As much as I like Brandon, I just HATE the way he and André act whenever they're around each other. They are both so IMMATURE!

Most of the time I feel like I AM their BABYSITTER! And they BOTH need to be put in TIME-OUT!

Sorry, but I have way more important things to do than referee their BRATTY little BATTLES.

Anyway, it's quite obvious that everyone is SUPERexcited about my party. But I STILL need to convince my mom and dad to pay for it.

My BFFs should be Skyping me again any minute now. If we really want this party to happen, we need to come up with a budget that my parents CAN'T refuse.

FINGERS CROSSED!

!!

THURSDAY, JUNE 12

OMG! The registration DEADLINE for the trip to PARIS was last night at midnight! I can't believe that I ALMOST completely forgot about it.

I went to bed around 9:30 p.m. last night. But at exactly 11:55 p.m., I woke up in a cold sweat and suddenly remembered that I hadn't sent in my Parental Permission Form yet.

My parents had signed it two weeks ago. And I'd already scanned it and attached it to an e-mail. But I'd never clicked the send button.

The CRAZY part was that I just sat there last night staring at the computer screen, like, FOREVER!

I guess I STILL wasn't really sure if I wanted to spend July in Paris or touring with the Bad Boyz.

But, at exactly 11:59 p.m., I FINALLY chose . . .

ME, FINALIZING MY SUMMER PLANS!

I'm NOT going to tell my friends just yet. I want to break the news to them gently, all at the same time. Maybe over pizza or cupcakes.

Anyway, today I planned to talk to my mom about paying for my birthday party. So I gave her a neatly typed and very detailed copy of the budget my BFFs and I had carefully made.

"Hey, Mom, here's a list of everything I need for my birthday party. And it's ONLY, um . . . $500."

I smiled nervously. . . .

ME, SHOWING MOM MY PARTY BUDGET

Mom closed her book and gasped like I had just
announced that I was running away to join the
circus and asked to borrow her credit card.

"$500?! Really, Nikki?!" she groaned. "Do you really
NEED to rent a POOL?"

"Wait! Before you say no, just think about it!"
I argued. "It's a lot LESS than what kids at my
school spend on THEIR birthday parties. MacKenzie
had hers at the country club!"

"You're NOT MacKenzie!" Mom exclaimed. "Her yoga
outfit probably cost MORE than my CAR! I think a
party in the backyard could be really fun and a lot
LESS expensive!"

I had to concede that my mom was right. But NOT
about a party in our backyard being fun and cheaper.

I'd ALREADY come to the conclusion that
MacKenzie's yoga outfit probably cost MORE than
Mom's CAR!

My mom didn't seem to understand that my party was a VERY important event! Chloe and Zoey said it could either MAKE or BREAK our reps at school next year.

"Listen, Nikki, let's just do a smaller birthday party this year and save up for a big one next year, okay?" Mom suggested. "I've already made a budget for you. It won't be an expensive luau pool party, but it'll be just as FUN."

Then she gave me her handwritten note. . . .

Nikki's Birthday Party

Pizza	$45
Kool-Aid	$5
Cake	$20
Ice Cream	$10
Partyware	$10
Decorations	$10
Total	$100

I could not believe my OWN mother wanted to spend ONLY $100 on my party!

Brianna's last birthday party cost at least $300! But most of that was to pay for broken dishes and other damage to the Queasy Cheesy restaurant. . . .

BRIANNA, THE PARTY ANIMAL!

I tried to explain to Brianna that just because she was the birthday girl didn't mean she could climb up on top of the table and start singing and dancing like she was Taylor Swift or somebody.

But she wouldn't listen.

Thank goodness Brianna wasn't hurt when the table tipped over and she landed right on top of Queasy the Mouse, who was serving pizza at the table next to ours. She hit poor Queasy so hard that she knocked the wind out of him and his plastic nose popped right off.

OMG! I was SO embarrassed!

Anyway, Mom suggested that we carefully review both of our proposed party budgets and continue our discussion tomorrow.

Sorry, Mom! But I DON'T need to review your stupid cheapo budget! I already know it'll NEVER work!

☹!!

There was just no way that Mom's $100 party budget was going to work. Chloe, Zoey, and I could easily spend that amount in ONE evening just on pizza, movie tickets, popcorn, soda, and candy.

I was waiting at the front door when my mom got home from work.

"Mom, I can't have an island luau party with only $100!" I whined. "And what about music? The DJ would probably cost more than that!"

"Well, how would you like to have LIVE music for your party instead of a DJ?" Mom asked.

I couldn't believe my ears!

"Are you serious?!" I exclaimed happily. "Mom, that's great! I have a list of three bands that Chloe and Zoey suggested. I'll contact them to see if they're available."

"Actually, I was thinking that we could just ask Mrs. Wallabanger," Mom said.

"You want Mrs. Wallabanger to contact the bands?!" I asked, a little confused.

"No, Nikki! She's been taking accordion lessons and offered to provide music at your party for FREE!" Mom explained. "And the best part is that she asked a couple of the ladies from her belly-dancing class to join her. Isn't that SWEET of her?"

"Mom, are you KA-RAY-ZEE?!" I shrieked. "I want a SUPERcool POOL party! Not a STUPID belly-dancing-polka party for OLD PEOPLE!"

But I just said all that inside my head, so no one else heard it but me.

Just the thought of our elderly next-door neighbor and her friends performing at MY party in front of all my FRIENDS made me throw up in my mouth a little. . . .

MRS. WALLABANGER, PERFORMING AT MY
BIRTHDAY PARTY WITH BELLY DANCERS ☹!

OMG! I was SO upset with my mom that I ran upstairs to my bedroom and slammed the door.

But I had no privacy WHATSOEVER because within sixty seconds Brianna barged in without even knocking.

She handed me a picture of a sloppily drawn birthday cake. . . .

BRIANNA'S CAKE FOR MY BIRTHDAY?!

"Guess what, Nikki? I can make you a birthday cake for your party! It'll have ALL your favorite foods and costs ONLY $200! Would you like to place your order?"

YES! My little sister, Brianna, who can barely fix herself a bowl of Fruity Pebbles cereal, had offered to bake the BIRTHDAY CAKE for MY party!

"Brianna, my favorite foods are pizza, ice cream, sushi, pancakes, clam chowder, and Skittles candy. WHAT kind of a cake will THAT be?!" I fumed.

"I don't know." She shrugged. "A very STRANGE but YUMMY one?!"

I did not appreciate her little JOKE!

My party was NOT a laughing matter!

"Brianna, you can't just throw random foods together like that. Your WACKY birthday cake could give my party guests a MILD case of FOOD

POISONING and a SEVERE case of DIARRHEA! What am I supposed to do? Hand out bottles of Pepto-Bismol and stomach pumps in my party goody bags?!" I yelled at her.

But the most disturbing part was that my very own sister was charging me the outrageous price of $200 for a NASTY pizza—ice cream—sushi—pancakes—clam chowder—Skittles—FLAVORED cake!

With only FOUR candles on it!

What a RIP-OFF!

Sorry, but little kids today have NO integrity!

Although, to be honest, I wouldn't want Brianna's cake even if it were FREE!

Yesterday Brianna baked me a cookie.

Only it didn't look like one, because it was shaped like a big blob and was kind of burnt.

It actually looked more like something she'd scraped off the floor of a monkey cage at the Westchester Zoo ☹.

OMG! Just being in the same room as Brianna's cookie makes me feel sick. . . .

ICK!

BRIANNA'S VERY NASTY-LOOKING COOKIE

I thanked her for it just to be nice. But as soon as she left the room, I tossed her so-called cookie right into the trash.

About an hour later I was surprised to discover that Daisy had snuck something out of the trash can and was happily munching on it.

BRIANNA'S COOKIE ☹!!

I tried to stop Daisy, but it was too late! She had eaten every last crumb.

"NO, NO, DAISY! BAD DOG!" I scolded her.

That's when Brianna rushed into the kitchen to see what all the commotion was about.

After I explained what had happened, Brianna looked really disappointed.

Then she sniffed sadly and muttered, "Well, at least SOMEBODY liked my cookie."

Yes, Daisy loved Brianna's cookie. But Daisy also loves to eat garbage and drink toilet water.

Although I felt sorry for my little sister, I have to admit that garbage and her cookie have a lot in common. Both are NASTY and need to be BURIED in a LANDFILL to protect the PUBLIC!

Anyway, THAT'S the reason why Brianna making MY birthday cake is a really, really BAD idea.

Between my mom's tacky, SUPERcheap party budget, Mrs. Wallabanger's accordion music with elderly belly dancers, and Brianna's nasty birthday cake, my party is going to be a . . .

TRAIN WRECK!

HOW am I supposed to have an exotic island luau POOL party in our backyard when we don't have a SWIMMING POOL?!! I guess I'll just have to HUMILIATE MYSELF and use Brianna's Princess Sugar Plum inflatable KIDDIE POOL for my party! . . .

ME, HUMILIATING MYSELF IN BRIANNA'S
PRINCESS SUGAR PLUM KIDDIE POOL!

THANK YOU, MOM!

The thing I've DREADED most since the first day I started planning this party has just happened.

I thought the person who was going to RUIN one of the HAPPIEST days of my life would be my FRENEMY!!

But my very own MOTHER has single-handedly turned MY birthday party into a complete . . .

NIGHTMARE!

And it's all YOUR fault!

!!

NOTE TO SELF: My cheapo parents have also decided that a new bike for my birthday will be too expensive! Even though I need one really badly. They told me to pick something else, so I'm going to ask for a CAN OF BAKED BEANS!! I am NOT lying ☹!

JUST GREAT ☹!

I barely slept at all last night!

And right now I'm pretty much FREAKING OUT!

WHY?!

Because I've got way too many problems.

First: I desperately need $500 to pay for my island luau birthday party.

Second: The woman who gave birth to me (yes, my OWN mother!) has HIJACKED my party and turned it into a SUPER-low-budget belly-dancing-polka party for senior citizens.

Third: I need to let Chloe and Zoey know that I'm seriously having second thoughts about all this party stuff.

Fourth: I'm starting to feel a little guilty because I still haven't told my BFFs and Brandon I'll be going to Paris instead of on the Bad Boyz tour with our band, Actually, I'm Not Really Sure Yet.

And what if they get MAD at me?! Our friendships could be RUINED!

Normally, I would handle these problems like an IMMATURE middle school student by having a complete MELTDOWN and SCREAMING. But now that I'm older and more mature, I try to remain cool and calm.

For starters, I did some positive thinking and carefully considered my options.

Then, to find my inner peace, I did some deep-breathing exercises.

Finally, to chillax, I took a long, relaxing, hot shower.

And after ALL that, I . . .

. . . HAD A COMPLETE MELTDOWN
AND SCREAMED MY HEAD OFF!!

Screaming in the shower really helped, and I actually
felt hopeful and more in control of my life.

Until I saw my mom in the hallway, and she gave me an update on all her party planning. . . .

ME, TOTALLY DISGUSTED WITH MY PARTY

Sorry! But I just CAN'T . . . !

I didn't think it was HUMANLY possible for my party to get any WEIRDER than it already was.

But, thanks to my mom, it just DID!

Instead of TWO elderly belly dancers dancing to Mrs. Wallabanger's accordion folk music, I now have TWENTY-FOUR of them?!!

AAAAAAAAAAHHH!!!

That was me SCREAMING again!

My birthday party is officially . . .

CANCELED!

!

My BFFs were really looking forward to my
birthday party.

So I knew they were going to be very disappointed
that I'd canceled it.

I left Chloe and Zoey the following message on
their cell phones. . . .

"Sorry, but I've got some really bad news. My
birthday party is officially CANCELED! As much
as I'd love to spend it celebrating with family and
friends, instead I'll be locked in my bedroom, sitting
on my bed in my pajamas, STARING at the wall and
SULKING! I hope you both understand."

Instead of a big birthday bash, I planned to have a
huge PITY PARTY ☹!

But hey! Why wait? I was feeling SO AWFUL,
I decided to get started on my STARING and
SULKING right away. . . .

ME, SULKING IN MY ROOM ABOUT MY
CANCELED BIRTHDAY PARTY ☹!

119

Which, strangely enough, always seems to make me feel a lot better ☺.

But my sulking plans were completely RUINED when Chloe and Zoey called me back on my cell phone.

"OMG, Nikki! We just got your message. You're totally stressing out over this party! Please CHILLAX!" Zoey said.

"Yeah, Nikki. Zoey and I have got this! We're going to plan EVERYTHING. All you have to do is show up! So please stop worrying," Chloe added.

"But you guys have no idea how messed up things are right now!" I whined. "My mom has taken over and turned it into a complete DISASTER!"

"Don't panic! I'm sure the situation is not as bad as it seems," Zoey exclaimed.

"I really appreciate everything you guys have done so far. But I think this party is a really BAD idea!" I muttered.

"Please, just listen, Nikki!" Zoey said. "Put on some SUPERcomfortable clothes. We know the perfect activity that will get rid of all your NEGATIVE energy!"

"Yeah, and when we're done, you're going to feel calm, happy, and TOTALLY relaxed! We'll be there in ten minutes," Chloe said.

"You guys are the best friends EVER!" I gushed.

I had no idea what they were planning, but I was already starting to feel a lot better. I was SO looking forward to . . .

Hanging out in my bedroom and bingeing on a gallon of cookie dough ice cream until we were laughing hysterically at all my problems.

Chillaxing at the spa while being pampered with chocolate face masks and mani-pedis as we munched on fresh strawberries.

Visiting the CupCakery to PIG OUT on some

DELISH red velvet cupcakes with cream cheese frosting. . . .

But I was WRONG! To help me CHILLAX, my friends took me on a very long and intense . . .

ONE-MILE RUN IN THE PARK! . . .

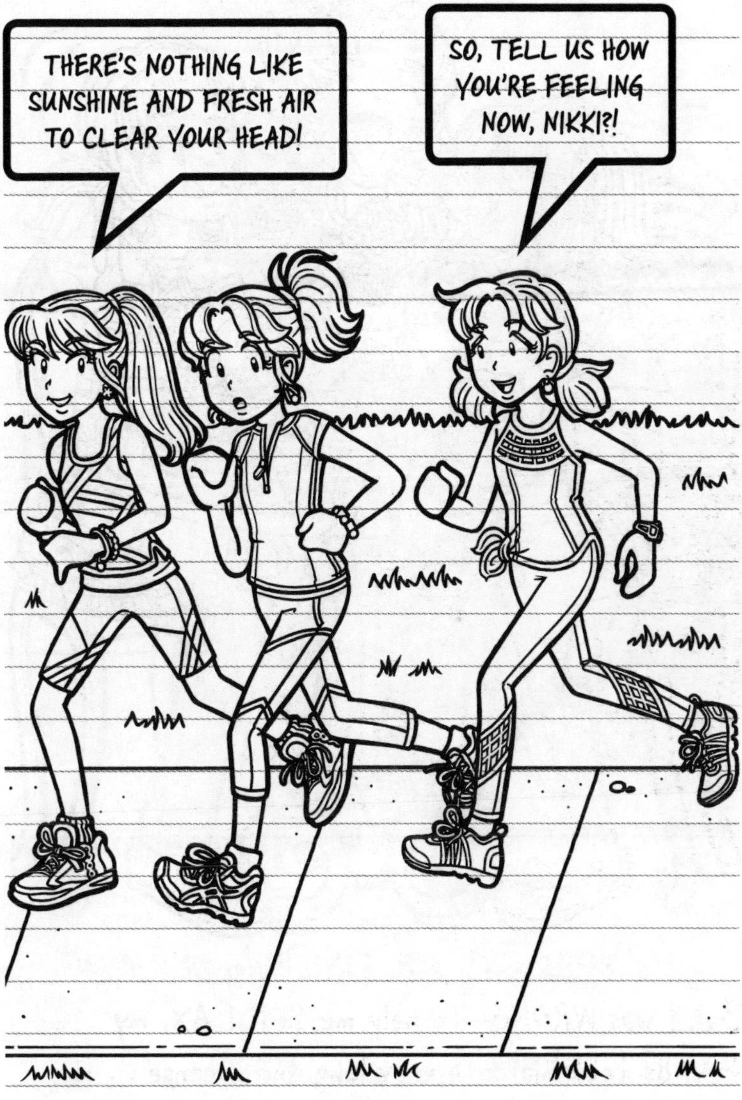
THERE'S NOTHING LIKE SUNSHINE AND FRESH AIR TO CLEAR YOUR HEAD!
SO, TELL US HOW YOU'RE FEELING NOW, NIKKI?!

MY BFFS AND ME, FINISHING OUR RUN!

Hey, I love my BFFs, but a gut-busting run in the park was NOT exactly what I had in mind.

It just aggravated an already BAD situation.

Not only was my party canceled, but now my stomach was on fire, every inch of my body ached, I felt dizzy, and I was about to throw up!

"Nikki, we'll ALWAYS be here for you! No matter what happens!" Zoey said.

"Now, do you want to tell us what's wrong?" Chloe asked.

Then they both gave me a big hug.

OMG! Right then I felt so frustrated and upset, I almost burst into tears!

UH-OH! I think I need to stop writing and go check on Brianna. It smells like she's cooking something again. I'll just have to finish this diary entry later!

WHY was I not born an ONLY child?!

☹!!

In my last diary entry, Chloe and Zoey had just asked me WHY I wanted to cancel my party. There were SO many reasons, I didn't know where to start.

"Well, my mom started planning things, and all her ideas are pretty CRUDDY! She wants to have it in the backyard. But how can I have an island luau party with no water?! It's not going to be any fun. So I just decided to cancel it. I knew this party was a really stupid idea to begin with. WHAT was I thinking?!" I ranted.

"WHOA! Just calm down, Nikki," Chloe said, grabbing my shoulders. "Don't say that! Birthdays are important! It's the one day a year that's all about YOU!"

"She's right," Zoey agreed. "A birthday celebration is too special to just cancel. If we work together, I'm sure we can fix all the problems. So let's hear the details."

"Well, okay! If you insist." I sniffed. "First, my mom slashed our party budget down to $100!"

"OUCH! Now that's a SUPERtight budget!" Zoey frowned. "It's barely enough for snacks."

"It gets worse!" I continued. "Brianna wants to make MY birthday cake. And I'm really worried my mom might actually let her do it if it'll save money!"

"How SWEET!" Chloe gushed.

"I think it's CUTE that Brianna wants to make your birthday cake!" Zoey giggled.

I shot them both a dirty look. "NOT if it's a pizza—ice cream—sushi—pancakes—clam chowder—Skittles—FLAVORED birthday cake! Because THAT'S exactly what she plans to make."

"EWW!" Chloe and Zoey gagged.

Just thinking about it made me throw up in my mouth a little. . . .

BRIANNA, MAKING MY BIRTHDAY CAKE!

"OMG! Would a cake with all those weird ingredients be safe for human consumption?!" Zoey wondered aloud.

"The hospital emergency room bills for your party could be INSANE!" Chloe worried.

"Well, Brianna's not even the BIGGEST headache!" I fumed. "Instead of a live band or DJ, my mom wants our elderly neighbor, Mrs. Wallabanger, to provide the music and perform with her backup dancers. Mom loves the idea since it'll be FREE!"

"REALLY?!" Chloe said. "I didn't know Mrs. Wallabanger was in a band. What does she play? And are her dancers hip-hop or street?"

"That's exactly the problem!" I grumbled. "Mrs. Wallabanger plays polka on her accordion!"

"POLKA?!" Chloe and Zoey exclaimed. "On an ACCORDIAN?!"

"And she has twenty-four belly dancers, including her best friends, Mildred and Marge!"

"BELLY DANCERS?!" Chloe and Zoey gasped.

"YIKES!" Zoey cried. "Just ONE of the things you mentioned is an instant PARTY KILLER! Sorry, Nikki, but it looks like your party is going to be MURDERED at least FOUR times!"

"I totally agree! And having all those dancing grandmas could be DANGEROUS!" Chloe scowled.

"Dangerous?! How?" I asked. "Like, one of them could fall and break a hip while they're dancing?"

"No! Dangerous because your party could end up on social media as 'THE WORST PARTY EVER!'" Zoey warned.

"Kids post and share videos of CRUMMY parties as a joke," Chloe said grimly. "You'd NEVER live that down! Socially, it's the KISS OF DEATH!"

Of course I wanted to have a birthday party.

But the LAST thing I wanted was to be known as the PATHETIC KID who had THE WORST PARTY EVER! How HUMILIATING! ☹ . . .

EVERYONE LAUGHING AT ME AND GOSSIPING
ABOUT MY VERY LAME PARTY!

Chloe and Zoey stared silently at me and then at
each other.

"Well, there's only ONE thing left to do!" Zoey muttered as she tried to muster a smile.

"Yeah. It sounds like YOU'RE thinking exactly what I'M thinking!" Chloe agreed.

I didn't quite know what they were thinking. But with their vast experience and expertise, I was VERY sure they could save my party.

I could ALWAYS depend on my BFFs ☺!

"Okay, Chloe and Zoey. Now that you've heard all my problems, what do you think I should do?" I asked hopefully.

I was totally shocked by their response!

"CANCEL THE PARTY!"
they both exclaimed.

"WHAT?!" I gasped. "Are you sure?!"

"Your situation is HOPELESS!" Zoey groaned.

"Your party will be a DISASTER!" Chloe moaned.

The fact that THEY were so upset made ME even more upset. My BFFs looked so sad, I thought they were going to cry.

"We're so sorry, Nikki!" Zoey sniffed.

"Maybe we can have a party for you next year," Chloe muttered.

"Come on, group hug!" I said, plastering a fake smile across my face. "I'm SO over this party!"

But as we left the park I suddenly felt a wave of despair and tried to blink back my tears.

When I first started attending WCD, I was pretty much a social outcast, and I NEVER want to relive that HORROR again. But somehow, what was supposed to be a fun birthday celebration with friends was being TWISTED into a shallow popularity contest and malicious social media event.

Why was this party stuff so COMPLICATED?! . . .

It's really sad! But sometimes kids can be so CRUEL!

☹!

Now that my party was canceled, I expected to feel happy, relieved, and thankful that I'd narrowly avoided an EPIC DISASTER!

But instead, I was feeling down in the dumps, disappointed, and depressed.

Chloe didn't help matters when she called me to ask what I wanted her to do with my invitations now that my party was canceled.

The thought of getting rid of them after all our hard work made me feel even WORSE. So I just sighed deeply and muttered, "Actually, Chloe, you can BURN them, SHRED them, or BURY them in your backyard! I REALLY don't care! I'm so OVER my party!"

Chloe was quiet for a few seconds. Then she said, "Um . . . okay, Nikki. But how about something LESS dramatic? Like, maybe just TOSSING them in the TRASH?"

"Sorry, Chloe! I owe you an apology. I guess I'm still grumpy about my party being canceled. You can just throw the invites away. And thanks!"

So I was totally confused when I got a frantic call from her later that afternoon.

"Hi, Chloe!" I answered. "I'm FINALLY feeling A LOT better. What's up?"

"Um . . . about those invitations . . . ," she replied in a shrill voice. "A funny thing happened in my kitchen today! I went to toss them in the trash just like we discussed. But then my cell phone rang. So I placed the invitations on top of the counter, right next to the trash can. I planned to throw them away right after I answered the phone! I REALLY did!"

"So WHAT happened?!" I asked impatiently.

"Well, I left the invitations right there on the counter. Then I walked away to answer my cell phone. It was in my purse in the family room!" . . .

CHLOE, LEAVING MY PARTY INVITATIONS
ON HER KITCHEN COUNTER!

There was a long and awkward silence. "AND . . . ?"
I asked. "Chloe, what happened next?!"

"And . . . my grandma was on the phone!" she replied.
"We talked for an hour about baking cookies, Judge
Judy, my plans for the summer—"

"NO!" I interrupted her. "I mean what happened NEXT to my INVITATIONS?"

"Well, when I came back . . . ," Chloe sputtered, "they w–were . . . GONE! I'm SO sorry, Nikki! It's like they just disappeared into thin air!" . . .

MY PARTY INVITATIONS DISAPPEAR!!

"I left your invites right next to our little mail holder that had some bills in it. The bills are gone too. And now I can't find the mail anywhere!" Chloe exclaimed.

"Wait a minute! You said that ALL of the mail is missing from the kitchen counter, even your family's mail that was in the mail holder?!" I asked.

"Yes! I have some really bad news, Nikki! I think one of my parents might have, you know, um . . . accidentally—"

"MAILED OUT ONE HUNDRED INVITATIONS TO A BIRTHDAY PARTY THAT I JUST CANCELED?!" I shrieked hysterically.

"Er . . . something like that! Sorry!" Chloe squeaked. "MY BAD!"

"Did you check your mailbox yet?!" I asked.

"That's a good idea!" Chloe said excitedly. "Maybe someone stuck the mail in our mailbox out front.

The good news is that our mailman doesn't come for another thirty minutes. Nikki, we're probably freaking out over nothing!"

"I hope you're right! I'll hold on while you go check your mailbox!" I said.

Chloe gave me a play-by-play over the phone. "Okay, I'm walking out the front door. I'm going down the sidewalk. I see our mailbox. Now I'm opening our mailbox and . . . ! AND . . . !"

CHLOE, CHECKING HER MAILBOX!

"And WHAT?! Are my invitations still inside?! CHLOE! Are you still there?! HELLO?! . . ."

Chloe finally finished her sentence. "AND . . . we can start FREAKING OUT AGAIN! Our mailbox is EMPTY! Your invitations are MISSING!!"

"NOOO!! This is a total NIGHTMARE!" My head was spinning. "I'm calling Zoey, and we're coming right over! We need to track down that mail and try to get it back! Before it's too late!"

Chloe tried calling her parents. But her mom's phone went straight to voice mail. And her dad was in an important meeting, so she left a detailed message with his secretary.

After I explained the situation to Zoey, she cleverly concluded that a large packet of one hundred invites would not have fit inside Chloe's mailbox. She guessed that Chloe's mom or dad probably deposited the mail into the blue mailbox closest to their home, which was about four blocks away. So the three of us agreed to meet there.

141

When I arrived, Chloe and Zoey were already at the scene. Chloe was visibly upset and on the verge of a meltdown. . . .

ME, TRYING TO PEEK INTO THE MAILBOX TO SEE IF MY INVITES WERE INSIDE!

"Oh, CRUD!" I grumbled. "It's too dark to see anything in there! Does either of you have a flashlight? Or a MATCH? I'm DESPERATE!"

Zoey raised an eyebrow at me. "Nikki, I know you're really upset and want all this to go away, but I'm pretty sure setting a mailbox on FIRE is a federal crime! I AGREED to help you find your invitations, NOT serve five years in PRISON with you!"

"OMG! WE'RE GOING TO PRISON!" Chloe yelled hysterically. "IT'S ALL MY FAULT!!"

I frowned. "Actually, setting the mailbox on fire wasn't exactly what I had in mind. But now that you've mentioned it, a harmless little FIRE would get rid of those PESKY invitations! . . ." I thought about it for a moment and then let out a flustered sigh. "Never mind! Bad idea!"

"I'm SOOO sorry! This is all MY fault!" Chloe whimpered. "I'll NEVER, EVER get distracted on the phone again! Unless Grandma starts talking about her SUPERdelicious triple chocolate chip cookies again. I can't help it, guys! I have a serious cookie addiction! And if we end up in PRISON, that'll be my fault too!! I'm such a HORRIBLE friend!!"

We tried our best to console Chloe. I know she means well, but whenever she gets riled up, she turns into a major DRAMA QUEEN.

A man walking his dog down the sidewalk paused to gawk at all the commotion.

"Nothing to worry about, sir! Nobody's going to prison!" I assured him. "My friend here just gets REALLY emotional whenever she . . . um . . . sees a MAILBOX."

Just as we were about to kick the mailbox, give up hope, and go home, we heard a woman's voice. "Excuse me, but do you ladies have a problem? Maybe I can help!"

The three of us turned around and GASPED! We couldn't believe our eyes. Standing right there beside us was a MAIL LADY!

And since she was an official postal worker, I was sure she COULD help us ☺! We excitedly explained how my invitations had accidentally gotten mailed out AFTER I had canceled my birthday party.

"What an AWFUL situation!" she said, shaking her head sympathetically. "I mostly just service the homes in this area. So, unfortunately, I DON'T collect the mail from these boxes. My coworker, Joe, does that. . . ."

Disappointed, my BFFs and I groaned loudly.

"BUT . . . ," she continued as she winked at us, "I DO have a KEY to the boxes. I'm really not supposed to EVER interfere with mail, but I can see how desperate you are. And I had something like this happen when I was your age! So, ladies, why don't we take a quick look inside THIS one?"

We squealed in excitement and held our breath as she stooped, inserted her key, and opened the large bottom panel of the mailbox. CLICK! I slowly peeked inside and . . .

. . . NEARLY FAINTED IN DESPAIR,
RIGHT ON TOP OF THAT EMPTY MAILBOX!!

"I'm sorry, ladies! This mailbox is empty!" the nice
lady said. "And even IF your invitations WERE in
here, Joe probably has them in his truck by now.

146

He picks up twice a day. Maybe he will feel sorry for you and bend the rules as well if he hears your story. He has a daughter your age!"

Zoey read the pickup schedule on the front of the box and tapped her chin. "It says 'Last pickup at 4:00 p.m.' So where is Joe right now?"

The mail lady looked at her watch. "Well, he usually takes a late lunch at Crazy Burger right after he picks up here. It's 4:45 now, so he might be there another fifteen minutes. Then he drops off mail at the main office. You don't have much time, so you really should get going!"

Chloe, Zoey, and I squealed happily and thanked the mail lady for all her help.

"I really hope you find those invitations! Good luck, ladies!" She waved.

My BFFs and I practically ran the entire three blocks to Crazy Burger. Once we arrived, we desperately scanned the parking lot for Joe's mail truck. Until . . .

. . . WE FINALLY SPOTTED THE TRUCK!

"There it is!" I screamed happily. We did a group hug and high-fived each other. But when we turned around just seconds later . . .

148

. . . THE TRUCK PULLED OUT OF
THE PARKING SPACE AND TOOK OFF,
WITH US IN HOT PURSUIT!

"STOOOOP!! PLEASE STOP!" we shouted.

In spite of the fact that we chased him across the entire parking lot, screaming like our hair was on fire, apparently Joe didn't see us.

"WHAT are we going to do NOW?!" I groaned.

"How about we order a triple cheeseburger with extra-large fries and a lemonade from Crazy Burger?" Chloe answered. "I'm STARVING!"

"Chloe, HOW can you be thinking of a BURGER at a time like THIS?" Zoey muttered.

"Sorry! Skip the burger!" Chloe said. "How about we order a CHICKEN or FISH sandwich?"

"Wait a minute! Didn't the mail lady say something about Joe returning to the main post office? It's just four blocks west of here. Maybe we still have a chance!" I said as we took off running again.

The post office closes at 5:00 p.m., and it was 4:59 as we dashed up the sidewalk toward the main door. I could not believe we made it! . . .

. . . JUST SECONDS TOO LATE!
THE POST OFFICE HAD CLOSED!

Of course I had a complete MELTDOWN right
there at the front door.

AAAAAAAAAHHH!
(That was me SCREAMING!!)

There was nothing else we could do. The invitations were gone! I felt SO helpless!

In the next forty-eight hours, one hundred guests would be getting birthday invitations to a party that had been canceled. And now I didn't have a choice but to publicly HUMILIATE myself by CANCELING it. . . .

AGAIN ☹!

AAAAAAAAAHHH!
(That was me SCREAMING a second time!!)

"I'm SO sorry, Nikki!" Chloe apologized again.

"You're obviously really upset, Nikki. We need to get you home right away!" Zoey said gently.

"So she can calm down and get some rest?" Chloe asked.

"No! Before she SCREAMS again and gets us ARRESTED for disturbing the peace!" Zoey replied. "That security camera is watching us!"

Suddenly Chloe froze and stared at her cell phone in shock. "My mom must have finally gotten my phone message because she just texted me."

"It doesn't matter now! It's too late!" I whined.

Chloe read the text out loud. It said:

> Hi, hon! Don't worry about the party
> invitations. They're NOT lost! Your dad
> dropped them off at the mail room in his
> office building. Luv you!

Of course that was really great news ☺! We excitedly rushed two blocks west to the office building where Mr. Garcia worked.

153

Unfortunately, the building's mail room had also closed at 5:00 p.m. JUST GREAT ☹!

I was SO exhausted! I wanted to give up and go home! But Chloe insisted on showing us a cool little mail room trick that she had discovered when she was a little girl. . . .

MAIL SLOT

PACKAGE SLOT

CHLOE, SHOWING US A TRICK?!

I had to admit, sneaking into the mail room through the package chute was a BRILLIANT idea ☺! . . .

MY BFFS AND ME,
SNEAKING INTO THE MAIL ROOM!

"Quick! Grab one of those orange vests and put it on!" Chloe whisper-shouted. "That way we can try to blend in!"

We each put on a vest and then just stared at the place in AWE with our mouths hanging open!

Chloe explained that this was the mail room for fifty businesses that had offices located in the ten-floor building complex, including her dad's.

OMG! There had to be thousands of pieces of mail in that room. How were we ever going to find my party invitations?!

Thank goodness, most of the mail room workers had already gone home for the day.

We managed to completely avoid the people still there by HIDING behind big stacks of boxes, DIVING into carts piled with packages, and DUCKING between shelves lined with letters.

We'd been searching for almost an hour when . . .

CHLOE, STUMBLING UPON THE INVITES!

OMG! We were SO happy and relieved that this HORRIBLE ordeal was finally over that we almost burst into TEARS!!

We grabbed the invites and headed straight for the exit door, running as fast as we could! . . .

MY BFFS AND ME, RUNNING FOR THE DOOR!

"I can't believe we actually found the party invitations!" I huffed.

"It took teamwork and brains to track them down!" Zoey puffed. "We were AWESOME!"

"It would have been a DISASTER if they had actually gotten mailed out!" Chloe added. "Like, WHO makes a stupid mistake like that?! Not US!"

"Only complete IDIOTS!" we laughed.

Unfortunately, we were so busy running, talking, and laughing, we didn't see a mail room worker. At the very last second, we tried to stop!

But Chloe accidentally crashed into Zoey.

Zoey accidentally crashed into me.

And I accidentally crashed into the mail room guy.

Then all FOUR of us accidentally crashed into . . .

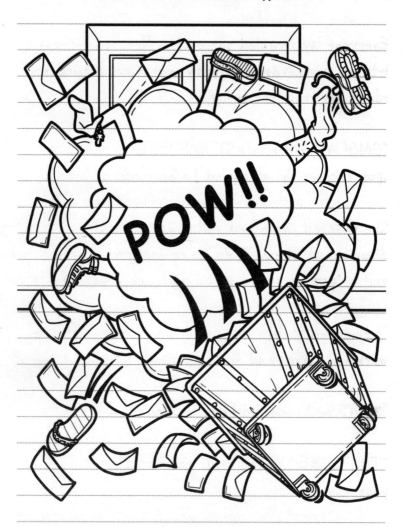

MY BFFS AND ME, RUNNING INTO TROUBLE
ON OUR WAY OUT OF THE BUILDING!

It was SURREAL!

Everyone lay sprawled out on the floor as business letters, postcards, and party invitations seemed to rain down from the ceiling.

"OMG! WH-WHAT JUST HAPPENED?" Zoey sputtered as she struggled to her feet.

She reached down and pulled up a slightly disoriented Chloe. Then Zoey grabbed my arm and helped me stand up on my wobbly legs.

"I think we accidentally collided with the mail room worker!" I muttered.

"WHAT mail room worker?!" Zoey asked.

"THAT ONE!" Chloe said, pointing at the poor guy.

We gasped! He lay motionless, buried beneath a huge pile of letters AND the mail cart. . . .

WE FINALLY NOTICE THE MAIL ROOM GUY!

That's when the three of us started to panic.

"OMG! WE JUST KILLED THE MAIL ROOM GUY!!"

Chloe shrieked. "Now we're thieves and MURDERERS!"

"Guys! This is really BAD! I feel like I've seen something exactly like this before!" I said.

"On one of those CSI crime shows?!" Zoey asked.

"NO! In THE WIZARD OF OZ!" I answered. "It looks like a tornado hit the mail room and clobbered this poor guy with a HOUSE! Just like that WITCH!"

"Except WE'RE the tornado!" Zoey said. "What should we do now?"

"Um . . . steal his shoes and WISH ourselves home like Dorothy did?" Chloe shrugged.

Thank goodness, the mail room guy wasn't DEAD.
How did I know?

Because he moved his leg and groaned, "Hey! Who
turned out the lights?!"

I felt kind of sorry for the guy.

One minute he was happily whistling show tunes as he
worked, and the next he was knocked into tomorrow
by a pack of psychotic birthday-party-obsessed girls.

We lifted the mail cart off him and quickly bolted
out of the room.

However, before we left, we took one last peek
through the mail room window to see if there was
any chance WHATSOEVER of us getting our hands
on those invitations again.

But they were loose, scattered, and completely
mixed in with the mail in that humongous cart.
Our situation was HOPELESS! . . .

CHLOE, ZOEY, AND ME,
LOOKING FOR MY INVITATIONS!

In spite of all our valiant efforts, my invitations got mailed out.

AAAAAAAAHHH!

(That was me SCREAMING again!)

Thanks to Chloe, my birthday party was ACCIDENTALLY back on again ☹!

I didn't think things could get any worse!

But on the way home Chloe, Zoey, and I got into a big argument about WHO was going to break the bad news to our one hundred closest friends that the party was NOT happening.

Sorry, but that sounded like the responsibility of my social director (Chloe) and my activities director (Zoey).

NOT the birthday girl (ME)!

There was only one thing worse than having to CANCEL my birthday party due to financial issues!

And that was having to **CANCEL** it **TWICE** because my invites ACCIDENTALLY got mailed out!

!!

NOTE TO SELF: Instead of completely humiliating myself and canceling my party, I should search the attic for Dad's old CLOWN SUIT that he wore to my birthday party when I was a little kid.

Even though the backside is probably badly burned, I could always put on the costume and run away to JOIN the CIRCUS!

I'm totally qualified for a job as a CLOWN because my LIFE is LAUGHABLE and everything I do is a TOTAL JOKE !!

WEDNESDAY, JUNE 18

Okay, this is probably going to be the LONGEST diary entry EVER!

A lot happened today, and I want to include all the details.

But I'll probably get a cramp in my hand if I try to write down everything at once.

This morning I woke up to the wonderful aroma of something baking.

It smelled like Mom's yummy, hot, buttered cinnamon rolls drizzled with frosting.

Only . . . three times BETTER!!

Since I was really hungry, I jumped out of bed, got dressed, and rushed downstairs to the kitchen.

But I stopped in my tracks when I saw a sign in the hall sloppily scribbled in crayon. It said . . .

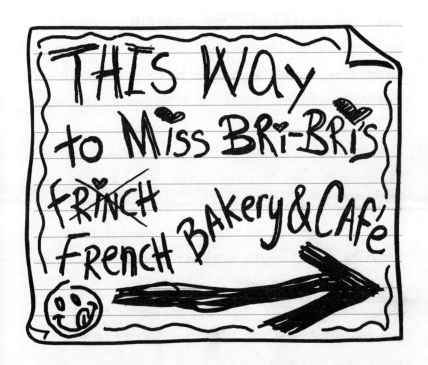

JUST GREAT ☹! I guess I WON'T be having any warm, tasty, freshly baked cinnamon rolls.

Unfortunately, whenever Miss Bri-Bri shows up, the ONLY thing I get a TASTE of is doom, gloom, and destruction ☹!

As much as I hated the thought, I didn't have a choice but to take control of the situation and confront her. BEFORE the COPS got involved!

Since Dad had to repaint the entire kitchen ceiling last week due to the damage from Brianna's sardine sandwich, we've made an extra effort to make sure she's ALWAYS supervised during her little cooking projects.

She's also not supposed to touch the appliances and other potentially dangerous items in the kitchen, including the spoons.

You'd be SHOCKED by how much damage my bratty little sister can do with a single spoon.

I've told Brianna a MILLION times never to put metal in a microwave!

But did she listen?

Repairing the charred black hole in the wall and replacing the microwave cost Mom and Dad a FORTUNE!

It was quite obvious to me that the sneaky little wannabe chef was trying to COOK UP trouble while we were all still asleep.

Brianna had decorated the kitchen with drawings of cookies and cupcakes and placed her kiddie-sized Princess Sugar Plum Teatime table and chairs in a corner.

She had also added her doll-sized table and chairs for extra seating.

Her dolls and stuffed animals sat at both tables, which were set with Mom's expensive china and fresh flowers from the backyard.

I was actually quite impressed. Her little pretend café almost looked like a miniature version of the CupCakery.

Brianna—I mean, Miss Bri-Bri—wore a cute pink apron with ruffles and bows, and a snarly frown on her face just like that mean British chef guy on TV who LOVES to yell at everyone.

However, as soon as she saw me, she quickly switched into "happy hostess" mode and plastered a huge smile across her face. . . .

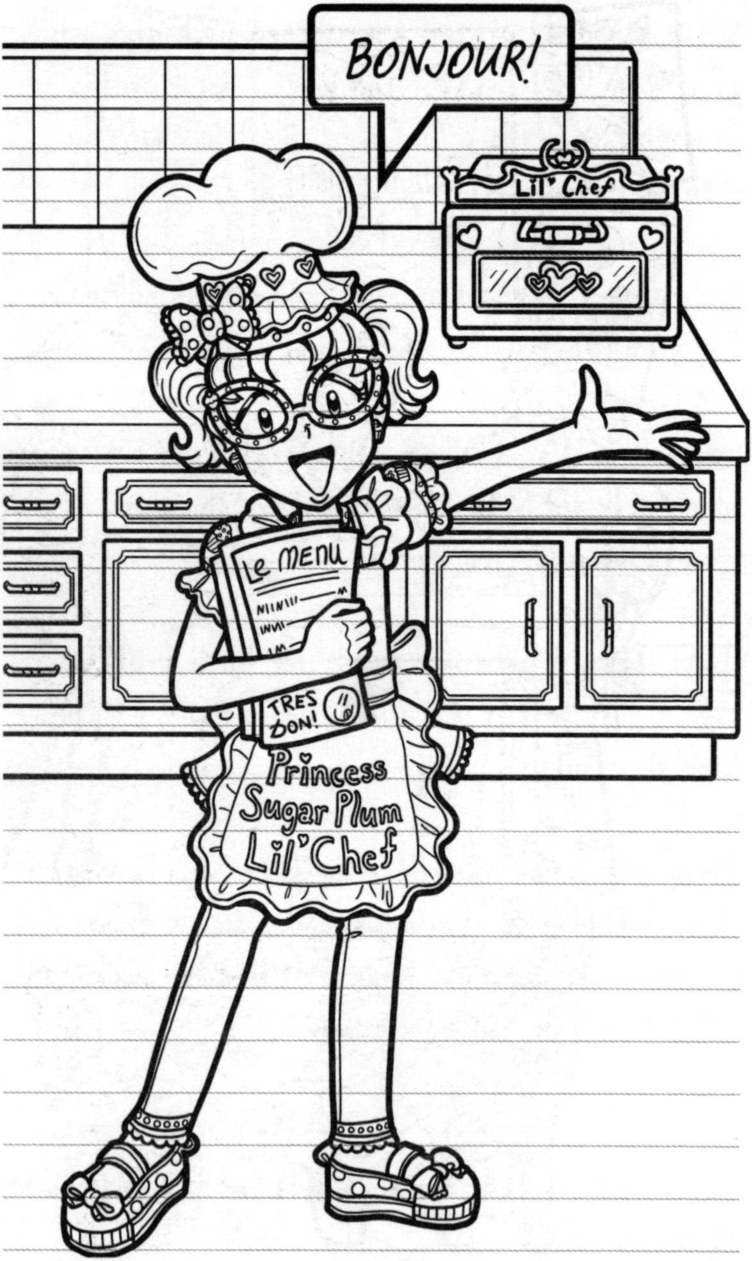
BONJOUR!
Lil' Chef
Le MENU
TRES BON!
Princess
Sugar Plum
Lil' Chef

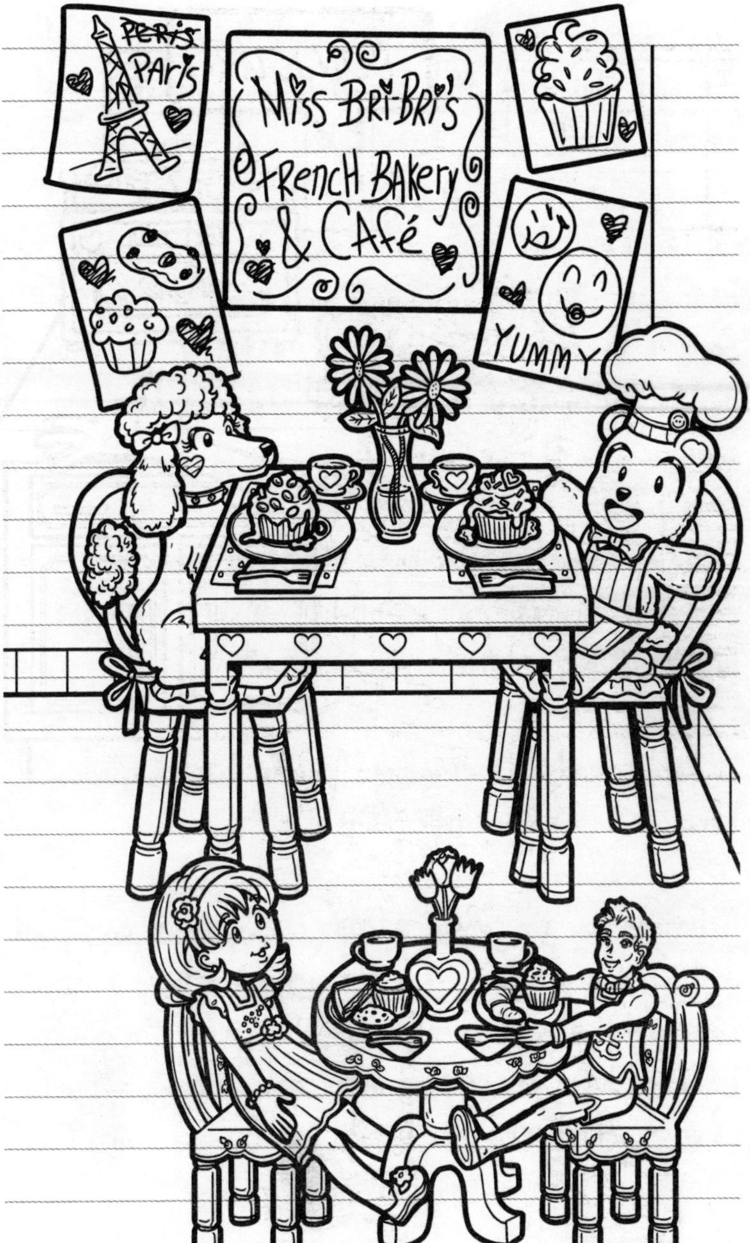

~~PERIS~~ Paris
Miss Bri-Bri's French Bakery & Café
YUMMY

"Welcome to Miss Bri-Bri's French Bakery and Café," she said, "home of Miss Bri-Bri, famous pastry chef to zee stars!"

"Brianna! WHAT are you doing?" I said, with my hands on my hips. "You know you're not allowed to cook in here ALONE. Especially after you blew up our second microwave and plastered your sardine sandwich on the ceiling!"

"I do not know zis Brianna that you speak of, dah-ling," she said, all snottylike. "And WHO might you be? Do you have a reservation?"

"I don't need a reservation!" I shot back. "I live here, and I'm your sister! DUH!"

"I believe you are confused, Miss Duh. I am an only child, and YOU are a CRANKY stranger! We have a strict no-cranky-strangers-allowed policy here in my café. I cannot have you scaring away zee customers. I will, however, check zee reservation list for you, Miss Duh."

Miss Bri-Bri flipped through her notepad.

174

"I see Barbie, Ken, Princess Sugar Plum, Doc McStuffins, Sparkle zee Poodle, Princess Shuri, and My Pretty Polly doll. But no Miss Duh," she said. "I am very sorry, dah-ling, but zee restaurant is completely booked today. So I must ask you to leave. Did you not see zee sign? It says 'RESERVATIONS ONLY!'"

She pointed at one of her signs taped on the wall behind me. . . .

"Really?! In what LANGUAGE?! I can't read your SLOPPY handwriting!" I complained. "And your spelling is terrible!"

"Well, excuse *moi*! Miss Bri-Bri eez a pastry chef, NOT a spelling bee champion," she huffed. "Anyway, zee rules are zee rules. If you'd like, I can put your name on zee waiting list. We might have an open table in about, um . . ." Miss Bri-Bri squinted and tapped her chin in thought.

"Well? How long?" I asked, slightly annoyed. "Ten minutes? Twenty minutes?"

"No! Longer than that. Can't you see I'm VERY, VERY busy?!" she exclaimed.

"Okay, then. ONE hour?!" I asked impatiently.

She sighed deeply and rolled her eyes at me.

Then she quickly scribbled something on her notepad, tore off the sheet of paper, and handed it to me. "HERE is your reservation time! Your table will be ready and waiting for you. Until then, GOOD-BYE, Miss Duh!" She smirked.

What LOUSY service! It took FOREVER just to get a reservation at this place!

And the café wasn't even that busy.

But when I realized how LONG I had to wait for a table, I was totally DISGUSTED! . . .

"WHAT?! Are you kidding me?!" I grumbled.

"Can't you read zee reservation card?! It says I'll have a table for you in THREE MONTHS! You will come back then, yes? Now GOOD-BYE!" Miss Bri-Bri said, shooing me out of my OWN kitchen like I was an annoying FLY or something.

There was NO WAY I was leaving her a TIP!

Okay, my hand is starting to cramp. And I need a snack. I'll try to finish this story tomorrow. ☺!!

When I left off, Miss Bri-Bri had just informed me that I had to wait a ridiculous THREE MONTHS for a table at her café.

Obviously, this was very upsetting news to me.

"**THREE MONTHS?!**" I shouted. "What kind of a shoddy café is this?! NO WAY! I'm staying right here to keep an eye on you!" I yelled. "Don't make me wake up *MOM* and *DAD!*"

"Calm down, PLEASE! No need to get THEM involved, dah-ling! Let me see what I can do!" Miss Bri-Bri said nervously.

She flipped through her notepad again and looked at the guests seated at her tables.

"Ah! You are in luck, Miss Duh! A reservation has just been canceled! Please follow me to your table!"

I glared at her. I didn't trust that lady at all.

Miss Bri-Bri snatched her doll out of a seat and carelessly tossed it over her shoulder. . . .

A TABLE SUDDENLY BECOMES AVAILABLE!

Yeah, right! HOW was I supposed to sit in such a teeny-tiny chair?!

"Thanks, but I'd rather sit on the floor," I said.

"Suit yourself, dah-ling!" she answered, obviously annoyed with me. "Now, here is your delicious appetizer. *Bon appétit!*"

Miss Bri-Bri plopped a plate of rubbery, burnt toast in my lap. THAT was NOT an appetizer!

If I just peeled off the crust, it would have made a perfect HOCKEY PUCK!

"Would you like to hear today's specials? Zee chef (that's me!) has prepared a PB and J sandwich, made with the world's finest, chunkiest peanut butter imported from a faraway place called . . . um . . . the grocery store. I also added crushed peanut shells for extra crunchiness!"

I gagged. "No thanks. Is anything on your menu actually edible?"

"I highly recommend Miss Bri-Bri's famous cupcakes. They're delicious, dah-ling! But it will be at least an hour before I can make one for you. My oven can only cook small batches at a time with its itty-bitty lightbulb. And right now I've got a very special delicacy baking."

"What is it?" I asked. "Is that what I smell?"

"Just eat your burnt toast—er, I mean appetizer—dah-ling! Then you must leave because I have VIP guests arriving very soon. Now please excuse me while I finish my pastries."

I watched in amazement as Miss Bri-Bri ran from one counter to the other, rolling out dough, cutting pastries, putting them into her oven, and piping frosting.

She actually looked like a real, fancy French pastry chef.

The incredible thing was that she did it ALL with her new Princess Sugar Plum Lil' Chef oven that I'd convinced Mom to buy for her. . . .

BRIANNA'S BRAND-NEW LIL' CHEF OVEN

Of course, now that Brianna . . . er, I mean Miss Bri-Bri, thinks she's a pint-size chef and foodie, it's probably going to create a whole new set of problems.

I'm all for new age parenting and encouraging kids to follow their dreams.

But let's keep it real!!

I never for one minute thought she'd actually be able to cook anything using two AA batteries and a one-hundred-watt lightbulb.

Her lazy assistant, Hans, was sitting at a table flirting with Sparkle the Poodle.

"Get off your lazy buns, Hans! Table One needs water and Table Two is still waiting for zee appetizer! Must Miss Bri-Bri do everything herself?!" she scolded her teddy bear assistant.

But Hans just stared back at her blankly, like he had cotton for brains.

"I swear, sometimes talking to you is like talking to a stuffed animal!" she ranted.

"Brianna, WHAT are you baking? I hate to admit it, but it smells wonderful!" I gushed.

I walked over to her oven to take a peek inside. As I reached for the oven door, she picked up a wooden mixing spoon and swatted my hand away.

SMACK!

"OW! That hurt!" I whined, rubbing my hand.

"NO PEEKING, dah—ling!"

Still! I just couldn't get over the fact that whatever she was baking smelled SO good, it made my mouth water.

And since I hadn't had breakfast yet and the hockey puck appetizer was inedible, I was practically STARVING!

Soon the timer on her oven went off with a loud
DING!

Now covered from head to toe in flour and frosting, Miss Bri—Bri put on a pair of pink oven mitts and pulled out a tray of the cutest little COOKIES. They were shaped just like the bow on her hat. . . .

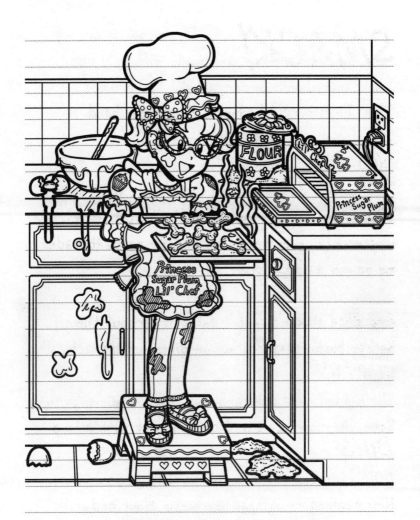

MISS BRI-BRI, BAKING COOKIES

Then she placed them on the kitchen countertop
to cool.

"Feast your eyes, dah-ling! These cookies are my very own secret recipe and made with only zee finest ingredients in zee world!" She grinned.

"Can I try one? PLEASE?" I begged.

"NO! Sorry, dah-ling! Zee cookies are NOT for YOU! They are for my special VIP guests. But today is your lucky day, yes? Miss Bri-Bri will allow YOU to be her taste tester."

"YES!!" I shouted, and I did a little boogie like I had just scored a touchdown or something.

She handed me a golden-brown sugar cookie with shiny hot-pink frosting on it. I couldn't wait to take a bite!

OOPS! My cell phone is ringing! It's probably my BFFs calling to discuss how we're going to notify everyone that my party has been canceled. Gotta go! More later! . . .

☺!!

FRIDAY, JUNE 20

Okay! So, I was DYING to try Brianna's cookies.

I nervously bit into one and held my breath.

It was crunchy, sweet, and buttery, and it practically melted in my mouth.

"MMMMMM, these are DELISH!" I moaned.

It was like I had bitten off a tiny piece of heaven.

"OMG! WHAT did you put into these things?!"

"It is a secret, dah-ling. If I tell you, I will have to kill you. With my cookie cutter. You will die a painful death of one thousand cuts!"

"Never mind!" I muttered as I took another bite. "Miss Bri-Bri! This is AMAZING!!"

"What's amazing?" my dad asked sleepily.

He and my mom trudged into the kitchen for their morning cups of coffee.

"You guys have got to try these!" I said, handing them both a cookie. "I can't believe I'm saying this, but I think your younger daughter is a cookie-baking prodigy!"

"*Bonjour!* I'm Miss Bri-Bri, zee legendary pastry chef to zee stars. Nice to meet you!"

She shook Mom's and Dad's hands like they were new guests at her café.

My parents winked at each other and played along.

"*Bon appétit,* dah-lings! Please enjoy your cookies." Miss Bri-Bri smiled.

Suddenly Mom and Dad didn't need coffee anymore.

The sensational flavor of those mouthwatering cookies shocked them awake like a Taser gun!

We couldn't get enough! . . .

WE LOVE MISS BRI-BRI'S COOKIES!

I had completely underestimated my little sister.

She was not only a very talented and creative chef, but a future gourmet GENIUS!

"I can't believe you MADE these!" Mom gushed. "I'm so proud of you, sweetie! We need to save your recipe! What did you use?"

"Well, sugar, cinnamon, butter, vanilla, rainbow sprinkles, Happy Dog Tender Kibble with Cheesy Bits, chicken gizzards, and, most importantly, my secret ingredient, Cap'n Crunch cereal!" Miss Bri-Bri beamed proudly.

At first we all just FROZE. Then, slowly but surely, the significance of Miss Bri-Bri's highly unusual ingredients started to sink in.

Even the weird shape of her cookies finally made sense to us.

Mom, Dad, and I gagged, coughed, and spit out our cookies at exactly the same time! . . .

MOM, DAD, AND ME, FREAKING OUT WHEN
BRIANNA TELLS US WHAT'S IN HER COOKIES!

I think all three of us felt a little nauseated.

Those cookies weren't shaped like little bows! They were bone-shaped DOGGIE treats!

Miss Bri-Bri was SO proud of herself.

"I call zem Miss Bri-Bri's Yummy Cookies for Dogs and Their Humans! They make your taste buds want to BARK, yes?!"

"My taste buds want to SLAP you with a SPATULA!" I yelled at her. "You just fed us DOGGIE TREATS without telling us!"

"This café has a very strict no-slapping-with-spatulas policy, dah-ling!" Miss Bri-Bri said nervously as she backed away from me.

"Is it WEIRDER that I just ate a doggie snack or WEIRDER that I want to eat another one?" Dad asked as he stuffed two more cookies into his mouth. "I can't get enough of these yummy things. I'm SO ashamed!"

"I totally agree, dear. They are DELISH!" Mom said as she snatched one out of his hand and popped it into her mouth.

I just stared at my parents. They were both snarfing down those doggie snacks like they hadn't eaten in weeks.

Suddenly, I came to MY senses.

"Mom! Dad! I can't believe you guys!" I yelled. "JUST STOP IT, PLEASE! YOU'RE HOGGING ALL THE COOKIES!"

I quickly grabbed some for myself before my parents ate them all.

"WHAT are you people doing?!" Miss Bri-Bri scolded us. "These cookies are for my two very important guests! A food critic from zee newspaper and a rep from zee French ambassador's office will be arriving very soon!"

"Yeah, right!" I scoffed as I popped another doggie treat into my mouth.

"I am VERY serious!" Miss Bri-Bri said as she whipped out her notepad and showed it to me.

I tried to read her sloppy scribbles.

"This morning a Mr. Brandon and a Mr. André made reservations for my café. They are friends of yours, yes?"

OMG! I almost fainted right there on the spot.

"They'll both be arriving here very soon, dah-ling! And if they LOVE my cookies, they'll give my café a five-star review. Then I'll be even MORE famous than I already am!" she giggled.

Miss Bri-Bri had invited BOTH Brandon and André to my house?!

I'm good friends with both of them. But they can't STAND to be in the same room with each other.

I totally FREAKED OUT and screamed . . .

Sorry, but I'm freaking out AGAIN just writing about all this stuff. I REALLY need to take a break.

I'll continue this diary entry tomorrow . . . MAYBE!

☹!!

Brianna has done a lot of TERRIBLE things to me during her lifetime. But inviting over BOTH Brandon and André and not bothering to tell me about it until the very last minute was a new low for her.

"How could you do this?!" I yelled at her.

"Actually, it was really easy. I just texted them," Miss Bri-Bri explained. "With YOUR phone."

"WHAT?! You used MY phone?!" I shrieked. "Now they're going to think I invited them here. Brandon and André practically HATE each other and can't stand to be in the same room!"

"Don't worry, dah-ling! You know what zay say, good food brings everyone together!" she said with a cheesy grin.

"It's going to take MORE than good food for those two to get along!" I grumbled.

"But zay ALSO say, nothing is more EXCITING to watch than a really good FOOD FIGHT between two people who HATE each other!" Miss Bri-Bri added cheerfully.

I started to PANIC! What if Brianna was right?! What if Brandon and André actually had a FOOD FIGHT?!

"Don't worry! There WON'T be any fighting." Miss Bri-Bri smirked. "Once Brandon and André taste the delicious cookies at my café, BOTH of them will FORGET all about YOU, dah-ling."

"Yeah, probably because they'll both be too busy FREAKING OUT over the fact that they just ate some DOGGIE SNACKS!" I shot back. "Thanks a bunch, Miss Bri-Bri. You've made a HUMONGOUS mess in the kitchen AND in my LIFE!"

Right then I was so angry at Brianna, I wanted to . . . SCREAM ☹!! But first I needed to contact both guys to let them know what was going on. Before it was too late!

I dashed up the stairs to my bedroom to get my cell phone, with Miss Bri-Bri in hot pursuit! . . .

I slammed my bedroom door and locked it. Then I grabbed my phone and started typing an e-mail as fast as my fingers could go.

That's when Miss Bri-Bri politely knocked.

"Listen, dah-ling. Let's make a deal! Miss Bri-Bri will clean up the messy kitchen and your MESSY LIFE! Yes?! Just don't touch zat PHONE!"

"Too late!" I said as I hit the send button on my phone. This is the e-mail I sent to Brandon and André. . . .

* * * * * * * * * * * * * *

To Whom It May Concern:

You are receiving this e-mail because you have just been scammed by a six-year-old wannabe pastry chef impostor who calls herself Miss Bri-Bri.

Please disregard this lunatic's text invitation to a five-star French bakery and café, as it is only a figment of her imagination.

I repeat, please ignore her message and STAY HOME!!

And, whatever you do, do NOT let her con you into eating her pretty pink cookies, which, strangely enough, are SUPERdelicious DOGGIE SNACKS.

WARNING!: Side effects of her cooking may include nausea, vomiting, confusion, dizziness, belly bloat, memory loss, severe acne, swollen feet, bad breath, tooth decay, intense itching, hair loss, uncontrollable diarrhea, ingrown toenails, and pungent body odor.

I apologize for any inconvenience my sister may have caused you. I am truly sorry and will spend the rest of the day locked in my bedroom trying to cope with the utter humiliation and sheer embarrassment of having to write this e-mail to you.

Your friend,
Nikki Maxwell

* * * * * * * * * * * * * * *

Within minutes, both Brandon and André responded to my e-mail.

Hey, Nicole,

So, the invitation to the French café isn't real? That's too bad. I really wanted a taste of home.

—André

What's up, Nikki!

I was worried your little sis, Brianna, was up to something! Thank you for the warning!

—Brandon

ANDRÉ AND BRANDON, E-MAILING ME BACK

"Your VIP guests just canceled," I told Miss Bri-Bri. "Now help me clean up this kitchen!"

"ARE YOU TRYING TO RUIN ME?!" Miss Bri-Bri shouted as she stomped around the kitchen throwing a temper tantrum just like those real chefs on TV.

We had finally finished up cleaning the kitchen and were about to put away her Lil' Chef oven, toys, and café stuff when we heard the doorbell.

Brianna rushed off to answer the door, and I collapsed into a toy chair and closed my eyes in exhaustion. I was still a little traumatized by all the drama she'd caused with her texts.

I must have accidentally dozed off or something, because all I remember is hearing a voice: "Welcome to Miss Bri-Bri's Café! Please have a seat. Would you like some lemon tea?"

When I opened my eyes, I expected to see Brianna serving tea to her doll or teddy bear. But it wasn't a toy at all. . . .

WHAT WAS BRANDON DOING
AT MISS BRI-BRI'S CAFÉ?!!

Brandon said that after reading my FRANTIC e-mail, he thought a cupcake would be the perfect thing to cheer me up. He even had one for Miss Bri-Bri! SQUEEEE ☺! . . .

BRANDON AND ME, HAVING CUPCAKES!

Brandon was RIGHT! That cupcake DID cheer me up. A LOT!

We just sat there kind of staring at each other and blushing while Miss Bri-Bri kept refilling our teacups with her delicious lemon tea.

But after her cookie recipe, there was NO WAY I was going to ask her what was in that tea to make it taste so good, because, honestly . . .

I DIDN'T EVEN WANT TO KNOW ☹!!

The last thing I needed was to completely embarrass myself in front of Brandon by SPITTING lemon tea across the room once I found out the weird, wacky, and slightly gross ingredients she'd used.

Anyway, I suddenly started to wonder if it was just me, or did Miss Bri-Bri's Café actually have kind of a romantic vibe?!

SQUEEE ☺!!

I was a little surprised when Brandon apologized for all the drama between André and him last week.

Then he said that he'd received his invitation in the mail a few days ago and was looking forward to hanging out with me at my birthday party.

I sighed and explained how the party had been on and off and on and off and then on again after the invitations accidentally got sent out.

And that I didn't have a choice but to contact everyone and let them know that the party was officially CANCELED. Again.

Brandon just blinked and looked REALLY confused about the whole thing. Although I totally didn't blame him.

Hey, it's MY party! And I'm STILL pretty confused about it TOO.

We were finishing up our cupcakes when Brandon cleared his throat and asked me a surprising question.

"So, Nikki, do you have any plans for dinner? I just got a FREE gift certificate for food that I won't be using. I think you can probably put it to better use than I can." He smiled.

"Wow! Thanks, Brandon!" I exclaimed. "Is it Queasy Cheesy, Crazy Burger, or someplace else? Hey! Maybe we can eat dinner there together?!"

Brandon tried his best not to laugh as he pulled the gift certificate out of his pocket and handed it to me. . . .

BRANDON'S GIFT CERTIFICATE
FOR MISS BRI-BRI'S CAFÉ!

However, after Miss Bri-Bri explained that her special of the day was a baloney and cheese sandwich topped with ice cream, ketchup, Goldfish crackers, and rainbow cupcake sprinkles, Brandon and I decided we'd just SKIP dinner.

Then we both laughed until we were gasping for air.

Even though most of the food at Miss Bri-Bri's Café was awful, we actually had a BLAST there.

As much as I'm looking forward to going to Paris this summer and spending time with André, I'm REALLY going to miss hanging out with Brandon!

I'm VERY lucky to have him as a friend!

☺!!

SUNDAY, JUNE 22

Today Mom and Dad went to the local Home Improvement Expo to promote Dad's pest control business, Maxwell's Bug Extermination.

Unfortunately, this meant that I now had my OWN pest control situation to deal with—babysitting Brianna for the entire day ☹!

I was chillaxing and watching a rerun of my FAVE reality show, *My Very Rich and Trashy Life!*, when I noticed that my house was unusually . . . QUIET!

(Well, other than the cast members hysterically screaming "I HATE YOU!" at each other and then, two minutes later, giggling insanely as they take selfies, smothering each other with air-kisses. I so LOOOVE that show!!)

Oddly enough, I heard no bathtubs overflowing, no smoke detectors screeching, and no Brianna excitedly shouting . . .

MY CELL PHONE HAS A TOILET FLOAT APP?!

WHAT was going on?! I decided to turn off the TV and find out!

Brianna wasn't in the family room watching cartoons, in her bedroom playing with her toys, or in the kitchen cooking up trouble with her Princess Sugar Plum Lil' Chef oven.

Daisy wasn't around either.

However, I did notice that her dog leash was missing from its hook near the front door.

This obviously meant that the two of them were playing outside in the yard, RIGHT?!

WRONG! There was no trace of them.

That's when I suddenly remembered Brianna mentioning that her best friend, Oliver, was visiting his grandmother, Mrs. Wallabanger, today.

And, just in case you were wondering, YES! It's THAT Mrs. Wallabanger! Our accordion-playing elderly neighbor with the belly-dancing BFFs, Mildred and Marge!

I rushed next door to Mrs. Wallabanger's house and rang the doorbell.

After what seemed like FOREVER, she finally answered.

I was surprised to hear dance music blasting inside the house. . . .

Boom-ba-da-boom! Boom-ba-da-boom! Boom-ba-da-boom! Boom-ba-da-boom!

Actually, the beat was kind of awesome!

Hey! If she'd play THIS kind of music at my birthday party, maybe I'd reconsider.

NOT ☹!

That was just a little joke, people.

Anyway, Mrs. Wallabanger was wearing leopard-print spandex pants, a brightly colored I HEART ZUMBA T-shirt, and sweatbands. . . .

MY NEIGHBOR, MRS. WALLABANGER!

"Hello, Nikki, dear! Sorry, but I didn't hear the doorbell right away!" she shouted over the music. "I'm doing a Zumba exercise video. It's so fun to boogie down! And would you believe that I'm learning to TWERP?!"

"Um . . . I THINK YOU MEAN 'TWERK,'" I yelled.

Her music was so loud, she could barely hear me, even with her hearing aid in.

Mrs. Wallabanger suddenly stopped smiling. "WHAT did you just say?! You THINK I'M A MEAN JERK?!" She scowled. "Don't get RUDE with me, young lady!"

"No! I didn't say that!" I shouted. "I actually said, um . . . never mind! Anyway, I'm really sorry to interrupt your workout, but have you seen Brianna?"

"WHAT did you say?!" Mrs. Wallabanger yelled.

"Could you lower the volume just a BIT? Then you can BOOGIE DOWN!" I yelled.

But Mrs. Wallabanger folded her arms and just glared at me.

"Well, I NEVER!" she huffed. "How dare you call me a BIG BOOTY CLOWN!! Now get off my property!!"

Then she slammed the door right in my face!

BAM!!

I just stood there staring blankly at the door as the music continued to blast.

Boom-ba-da-boom! Boom-ba-da-boom!

Since I was still on Mrs. Wallabanger's property, I decided to check her backyard. I was praying I'd find Brianna and Oliver playing together.

But no luck!

As I walked back to my house I noticed what looked like a random trail of crumbs.

Actually, PINK CRUMBS! It led down our driveway, out to the sidewalk, past our mailbox, and then disappeared.

Okay, now I was REALLY starting to PANIC!

I resisted the urge to call my parents and scream,

"MOM! DAD! BAD NEWS! BRIANNA HAS BEEN KIDNAPPED BY THAT CANDY WITCH FROM THE HANSEL AND GRETEL FAIRY TALE!! HOW DO I KNOW? IT LOOKS LIKE BRIANNA TRIED TO LEAVE A TRAIL OF CRUMBS TO FIND HER WAY BACK

HOME! BUT DAISY MUST HAVE EATEN THEM! WHAT?! NO, THIS ISN'T A PRANK CALL . . . !!"

Instead, I took a few deep breaths and tried to calm down.

Okay, if I were Brianna and Daisy, WHERE would I go and WHAT would I do?

I had to get inside their little heads. You know, think like a young, rambunctious, untrained animal and a cute little playful puppy.

I also had to consider that one of them loves to play in the park with friends. And the other loves to romp around chasing dogs until completely exhausted and then secretly pee in the grass when I'm not looking.

OMG!

That always drives me CRAZY!

No matter how many times I SCOLD Brianna about the importance of using the bathroom BEFORE we go to the dog park, she NEVER listens!

She'd been nagging me to take her to the dog park for the past three days. But ever since that mix-up with the invitations, I've been SUPERbusy addressing postcards to cancel my—

Wait a minute! Was THAT the answer?!

The . . . DOG PARK?!

OMG!

BRIANNA AND DAISY PROBABLY WENT TO THE DOG PARK!!

I practically ran the entire three blocks.

If Brianna WASN'T there, I wouldn't have a choice but to call my parents and alert them that she was missing.

Once I arrived, I didn't see Brianna or Daisy anywhere.

But there was a large crowd gathered near the drinking fountains. Sometimes local pet stores would hand out free samples of new products in that area.

Whatever was going on, everyone seemed to be SUPERexcited about it.

Not only were there a number of people in a long line with their dogs, but an even larger crowd had gathered around a small display.

Since I couldn't see very much through the mob of people, I decided to climb up on a nearby picnic table.

I took one look and almost FAINTED. . . .

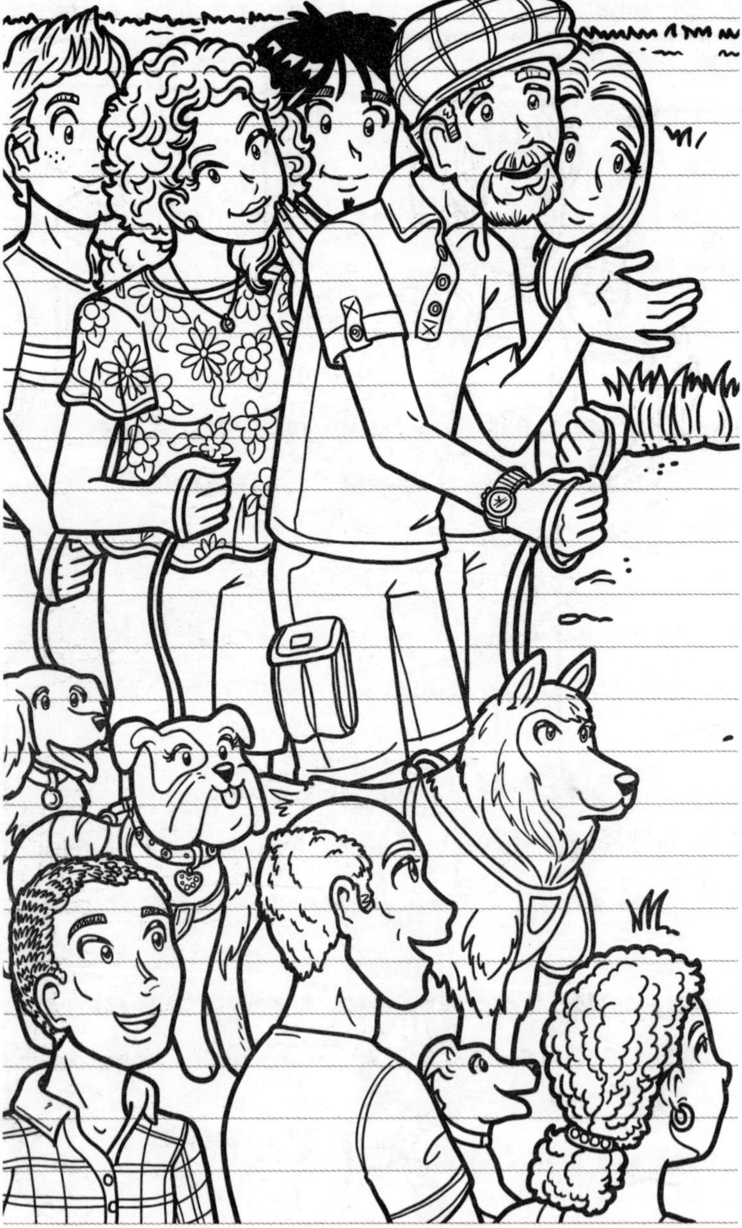

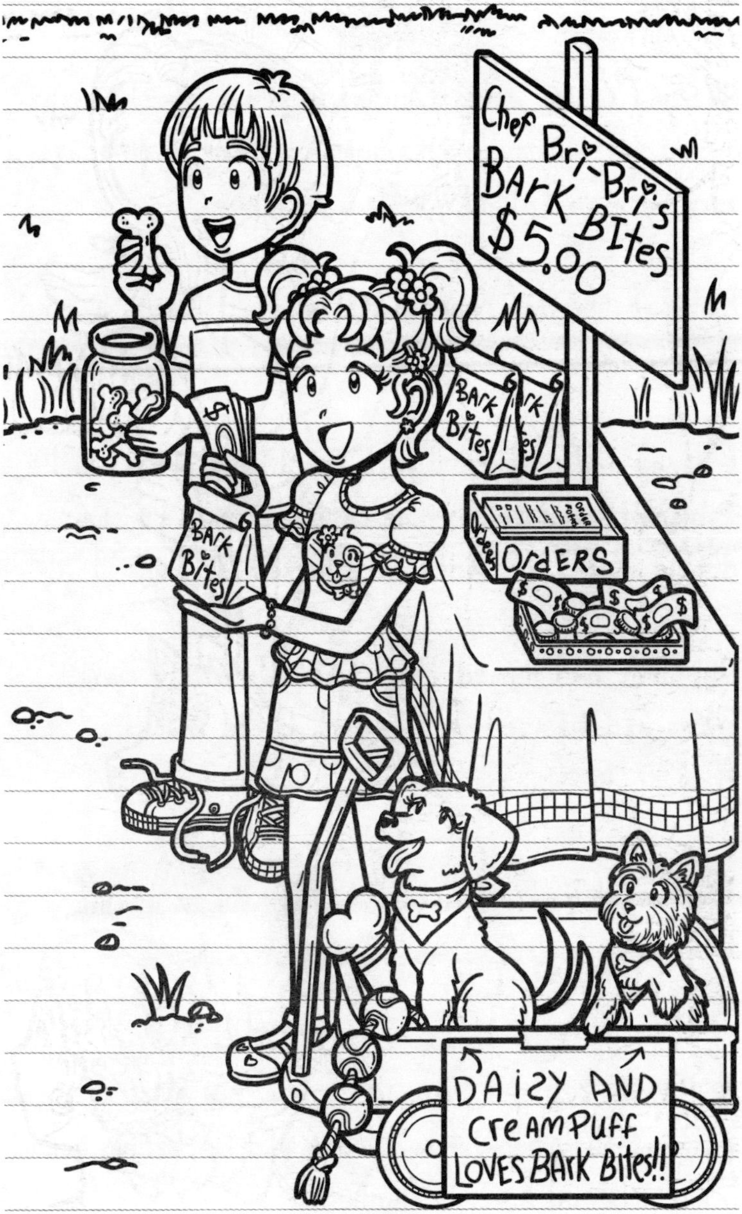
Chef Bri-Bri's
BARK BItes
$5.00
BARK Bites
BARK Bites
ORDER FORMS
Orders
ORDERS
DAIZY AND
CreAMPuff
LOVES BARK Bites!!!

It was BRIANNA!!

She and Oliver were standing in front of the large crowd with Daisy and Creampuff (Mrs. Wallabanger's very mean and slightly crazy Yorkie)!

Both of the dogs wore matching pink scarves around their necks.

Brianna had covered a park bench with Mom's pink tablecloth and set up the cutest display for her doggie snacks, complete with homemade signs.

Only, she had named them Chef Bri-Bri's Bark Bites and was selling a bag of three snacks for $5.00.

Yes, $5.00!

It was UNREAL!!

NORMAL kids sell lemonade for 25¢ a glass. Brianna was a miniature business tycoon and marketing genius in pigtails and a puppy shirt.

Oliver was handing out samples to people and their dogs. And after one bite, BOTH were literally BEGGING for more!

Daisy and Creampuff were busy charming customers with their adorable cuteness. And Brianna was handing out LITTLE bags of Bark Bites and collecting BIG wads of cash!

Hey, I'm all for little kids having big dreams. But NOT if they're tricking unsuspecting victims into spending their hard-earned money to eat doggie treats that are probably NOT all that healthy for HUMANS or DOGS!

I had a really bad feeling that this was NOT going to end well! As Brianna's older sister, I didn't have a choice but to put a stop to this before she got in WAY over her head!

I tried to squeeze through the crowd to get to Brianna, but I was blocked by a big pudgy man and his big pudgy bulldog. They both scowled at me with their big floppy jowls. . . .

"Hey, you! No cuts!" the man snarled. "I don't care how badly you want your Bark Bites! The line starts back there! Now take a hike!" He pointed to the end of a long line of about thirty people.

"Um . . . actually, I'm NOT here to wait in line for Bark Bites," I stammered.

That's when a prissy lady with curly, poofy hair and a curly, poofy-haired dog glared at me. . . .

I DIDN'T KNOW WHO WAS SNOBBIER, THE LADY OR HER DOG!

"I'm sorry, young lady. But you're just going to have to WAIT your turn like the rest of us! Cupcake and I have been patiently standing in this line for twenty minutes!" she scolded me.

"You don't understand. I'm NOT trying to cut in line for Bark Bites," I said. "That little girl is my SISTER, and I just need to talk to her!"

The man scoffed at me. "Nice try, kid! That's the same thing that teenager with the Chihuahua in her purse said. Only, I'm not falling for that sneaky trick again. Now SCRAM before Meatball here gets upset!"

Meatball growled, licked his chops, and then stared at me like I was a human-sized, um . . . meatball or something. YIKES ☹!!

"Hey, Nikki!" Oliver shouted happily as he waved. "It's a good thing you're here! I think Brianna could use some help!"

I rolled my eyes at the two grumpy people in line and rushed over to Brianna and Oliver.

"Here you go, lady!" Brianna handed a customer her very last bag of Bark Bites. "I hope you AND your dog enjoy them!"

"We already DID!" the woman said, practically drooling. "We ate the first bag and LOVED 'em! I'm glad we made it back to the park to buy more before you sold out!"

"SOLD OUT! What do ya mean, SOLD OUT?!" the guy with the bulldog yelled. "YOU GOTTA BE KIDDING ME!"

"YOU CAN'T BE SOLD OUT! CUPCAKE WILL BE SO VERY DISAPPOINTED! I PROMISED HER BARK BITES!!" the prissy lady screeched.

The crowd erupted into a loud chorus of groans, gripes, and grumbles.

Then they started to chant, "WE WANT BARK BITES!! WE WANT BARK BITES!!"

My initial reaction was to get the heck out of there. Sorry, but I'm very ALLERGIC to ANGRY MOBS!

The only reason I stayed was because my parents were NOT going to be happy at dinner tonight when

I explained to them that I'd left Brianna at the dog park with a large pack of wild, ferocious animals.

NOT the DOGS!

Their OWNERS ☹!

I cautiously took a few steps toward the angry mob and shouted as loud as I could.

"Everyone, please listen! I'm really sorry, but all the Bark Bites have been sold! This business is now closed. PERMANENTLY!"

"Says WHO?!" Brianna shot back. "You're NOT the boss of me, Nikki! We're not out of business until I SAY we're out of business!"

Then she climbed on top of the table to address her horde of disgruntled customers.

"Hey, people! Can I have your attention? You can STILL get your delicious Bark Bites! Just fill out an order form and I'll get them to you ASAP.

Or you can buy them . . . online at my . . . er, website, Chef Bri-Bri's Bark Bites!" . . .

BRIANNA, ANNOUNCING HER NEW
BARK BITES BUSINESS?!

229

I couldn't believe my sister was LYING to all those people like that. She did NOT have a website.

Heck, she didn't even know how to SPELL "website"!

I shot her a dirty look and hissed under my breath, "Brianna! WHAT are you talking about?! You DON'T have a website!!"

She giggled nervously, cleared her throat, and continued. "Um . . . actually, I meant to say, you can visit my Chef Bri—Bri's Bark Bites website, which I'll be opening. One day. Very soon. Probably!"

Then she plastered an innocent smile across her face and shrugged like she was just a little confused about the whole website issue.

The entire crowd erupted into cheers!

Then there was a wild stampede to the stack of order forms that Brianna had written in her sloppy handwriting.

Oliver, Brianna, and I had to dive behind the table to avoid the wild crush of happy humans and delighted dogs.

We gave out order forms until all of them were gone.

Then people started handing us small scraps of paper so we could write down the name of Brianna's nonexistent website.

That she was going to open.

One day. Very soon.

Probably!

People were so desperate to get their hands on Chef Bri-Bri's Bark Bites that many of them actually prepaid for their orders.

By the time the large crowd finally cleared out, Brianna's little red wagon was overflowing with five-dollar bills.

OMG! It looked like she had robbed a bank or something! . . .

BRIANNA'S WAGONLOAD OF MONEY!

Luckily, Brianna had brought her backpack, so we stuffed the money and order forms inside it.

Honestly, I have no idea how Brianna plans to fill all those orders for Bark Bites. And she needs a website, like, YESTERDAY!

As much as I'd LOVE to help her, I have my own problems to deal with.

Maybe Mom will help her out. Or it could be the perfect project for her Scout troop to earn their kiddie business tycoon merit badges.

Anyway, tomorrow Chloe, Zoey, and I will meet to work on the postcards we'll be sending out to all my guests to let them know that my birthday party has been canceled.

Zoey says that if we mail them out no later than Tuesday, everyone will have them by Thursday.

Then this birthday nightmare will finally be over!

Trying to come up with a letter to explain why my birthday party was being CANCELED was a lot harder than I thought it would be. . . .

Dear *Insert Name of Party Guest*,

I am very sorry to inform you that, due to circumstances beyond my control, my birthday party has officially been canceled. I sincerely apologize for any inconvenience this may have caused and assure you that I'm actually doing everyone a HUGE favor. Eating a slice of my nasty pizza—ice cream—sushi—pancakes—clam chowder—Skittles—flavored birthday cake while being forced to watch a bunch of little old ladies belly dance to accordion music would have more than likely induced projectile vomiting along with irreversible psychological trauma. If you have any questions, complaints, or just want to yell at someone for totally ruining your weekend, please feel free to contact my social director, Chloe Garcia.

Sincerely,
Nikki Maxwell

Okay, I'll admit my letter was a little harsh. To CHLOE! Although it was HER fault the invites had gotten mailed out, throwing her under the bus by making her deal with the birthday BACKLASH was probably unfair.

"Bonjour, dah-ling!" A familiar voice interrupted my thoughts. JUST GREAT ☹! . . .

IT WAS CHEF BRI-BRI! AGAIN!

"WHAT are you doing here in MY café? Do you have a reservation?" she asked rather rudely.

"Actually, the last time I checked, I was sitting at the table in MY kitchen," I shot back.

"No, dah–ling, THIS is a business! And we have a very strict NO–LOITERING–ALLOWED policy. So unless you want to request a reservation, GOOD–BYE! SORRY!"

I just rolled my eyes at her. I REFUSED to wait three months for a table. "No thanks. I'm leaving!" I answered.

"WAIT!" she said. "Let's make a deal. I really need a website. If you make one for me, I'll pay you with Bark Bites AND you can hang out in my café. Zat sounds like a good deal, yes?"

"NO!" I grumped. "I'm out of here! SORRY!"

"WAIT!" she said again. "What if I pay you with . . . MONEY?"

She reached into her pocket, pulled out a stack of five-dollar bills, and waved it right in front of my face, back and forth and back and forth like she was trying to hypnotize me or something.

Suddenly, Chef Bri-Bri had my undivided attention!

"Um . . . OKAY! I'm listening!" I muttered.

"Everyone LOVES my delicious Bark Bites! Dogs AND humans can't resist them," Chef Bri-Bri explained. "I'm going to be SO rich that I can buy a BABY UNICORN! But I need a business partner. If you help me, YOU can be SUPERrich too, dah-ling!"

Actually, THAT was the most RIDICULOUS thing I'd ever heard.

I realize we all have hopes and dreams, including my bratty little sister. But COME ON! Some things are just beyond the realm of possibility.

Everyone knows BABY UNICORNS don't exist! . . .

237

BRIANNA BUYS A BABY UNICORN?!

The only thing MORE unbelievable than this was the fact that I'd just been offered an opportunity to make some cold hard cash. I pulled out my calculator and quickly added up all the Bark Bites money and orders. It was a total of $970! After expenses, if we split the money fifty-fifty, we'd each have a profit of about $400.

OMG! That was enough money to pay for the swimming pool and almost everything else for my birthday party ☺! And maybe we can sell even more!

"Okay, Chef Bri-Bri! You've got yourself a deal!"

She gave me a firm handshake and a big smile.
"Welcome to the Bark Bites business, dah-ling!"

I took a cute photo of Daisy with my phone and had
a website up and running in about an hour. . . .

CHEF BRI-BRI'S BARK BITES WEBSITE!

Brianna and I spent the rest of the day diligently working together on our new business.

We rode our bicycles to the store to purchase ingredients and small plastic bags, ribbon, labels, and small boxes.

Back at home, while she baked with her Lil' Chef oven, I used the much larger kitchen oven. Each cookie sheet held two dozen snacks, so it only took a few hours to bake and frost enough doggie snacks to fill all the orders.

The final step was to get them ready to be mailed to customers.

I printed mailing address labels on the computer, and then we placed the bags of doggie snacks into boxes.

Somehow, Brianna ended up with more mailing labels stuck on her than on the shipping boxes.

Daisy helped out too and cleaned up any snacks that we accidentally dropped on the floor! . . .

DAISY, HELPING OUT
BY KEEPING THE FLOOR CLEAN!

Our Bark Bites business venture was a lot of work, but I decided to look on the bright side.

Every order I boxed up was another step closer to my SUPERamazing, SUPERepic PAR-TAY!!

It was Brianna's idea to check our new website to see if any more orders had come in.

We were shocked to see that a dozen new orders had been placed in just the few hours since the website had been set up.

SQUEEEEEE ☺!!

By the time my mom got home from work, everything was ready to be mailed.

And get this! She actually said she was really PROUD of our teamwork!

I was SO relieved Mom wasn't MAD that we'd set up a whole business without asking first if it was okay.

Plus, we needed her PayBuddy account password so we could process the orders from everyone!

Mom offered to mail off the orders for us at the post office on her way to work tomorrow morning.

This was really good news because I never wanted to see another mail room AGAIN!

Especially since I STILL had nightmares about Chloe, Zoey, and me crashing into that mail room worker! We'd literally knocked the poor guy right out of his shoes!

Anyway, as planned, my BFFs came over after dinner to help me write out the postcards to CANCEL my party.

They were understandably a little grumpy about the whole thing.

I could barely contain my excitement about the huge SURPRISE I had for them! . . .

ME, SHOWING MY BFFS THE CASH
TO PAY FOR MY BIRTHDAY PARTY!

Chloe and Zoey were so shocked and happy, they
started screaming!

We did a group hug and excitedly resumed our party planning.

I now have enough cash for the swimming pool payment, which is due on Wednesday.

Although Chef Bri-Bri, pastry chef to the stars, is a little KA-RAY-ZEE, I'm happy she offered me a business deal I couldn't refuse.

I'm really proud of my little sister! I'm sure she's going to be a millionaire by the time she's ten years old!

Since my party is back on again, my BFFs and I decided to meet at the Party Palace tomorrow at noon to shop for decorations and supplies.

I'm SO excited, I can hardly wait!

SQUEEEEEEE!!

!!

TUESDAY, JUNE 24

Every time I visit the Party Palace, I'm totally AMAZED! Not only is it a HUMONGOUS store, but it has EVERY party theme imaginable!

For EVERY occasion!

For EVERY age group!

In just about EVERY color!

And today we were shopping there for MY birthday party! SQUEEEEE ☺!!

I had decided to drop off the payment for the swimming pool on my way to the store when I ran into my friend Violet.

When she found out I didn't have a DJ for my party yet, she actually offered to do it as a special birthday gift to me!

I was SO happy, I gave her a big hug! Violet has an

AWESOME collection of all the coolest music, and she was the DJ for our big Halloween party at school.

Anyway, thanks to our booming Bark Bites sales and my mom generously agreeing to pay for the cake, punch, pizza, and snacks, my BFFs and I now had $200 (safely tucked in my back pocket) to spend on cool decorations and partyware.

Near the entrance of the store was a large display of KA-RAY-ZEE party hats. Chloe and Zoey grabbed a huge plastic crown with colorful, blinking lights that blasted the "Happy Birthday" song, and they DARED me to wear it!

Hey! Compared to the humiliation I suffered at school every day, wearing a stupid hat was easy. I put it on, and the three of us took a hilarious selfie doing duck lips!

Zoey found a shopping cart, and Chloe and I hopped on. Then we zoomed through the store, giggling hysterically as I sang along to the corny music from my crown. . . .

MY BFFS AND ME, SHOPPING FOR MY PARTY!

The beach party section of the store was really colorful and covered an entire aisle. I just stared at the various displays in AWE! I had no idea there were so many different beach party themes, like Tropical Paradise, Surfer, Mermaid, Sea Creatures, Survivor, *Moana*, and Deserted Island, just to name a few.

"WOW! Look at all this AMAZING stuff!" Chloe exclaimed.

"So, Nikki, which party theme do you like best?" Zoey asked. "All of them are AWESOME!"

"Actually, I don't have the slightest idea!" I gushed. "HELP! I can't make up my mind!"

Chloe tapped her chin. "Well, do you want cute, cool, classy, edgy, chic, artsy, retro, or glam?!"

"Come on, guys. Just CHILLAX! We're planning a birthday party, not a rocket launch to Mars!" Zoey teased as we admired a SUPERcute grass skirt and flower headband. . . .

THE PARTY STUFF WAS AWESOME!

We decided the Tropical Paradise party theme was the best match to our invitations.

Lucky for us, the store manager suddenly announced a "buy-one-get-one-FREE!" sale on all themed partyware.

"OMG! I LOVE this stuff!" I said. "And now that everything is on SALE, we can buy TWICE as much! Come on, guys, let's shop till we drop!"

Chloe ran to get another shopping cart while Zoey and I frantically grabbed items off the shelves.

It was a mad rush as shoppers swooped into the aisles like hungry vultures. Within minutes, most of the beach party shelves were bare.

But my BFFs and I had TWO shopping carts loaded with cool stuff! We had a total BLAST shopping for my party ☺!

Finally, we headed for the checkout line to pay for everything.

As we waited in line, I reached into my back pocket to take out the $200. And that's when I had a COMPLETE MELTDOWN! . . .

Yes! My money had disappeared into thin air!

Just writing about all this is mentally exhausting. So I'll finish this entry tomorrow!

This whole party thing has been a never-ending, gut-wrenching . . .

ROLLER-COASTER RIDE!

And just when you think the ride is finally over and it's safe to get off, it spins you around until you're dizzy, dangles you upside down in midair until you feel like you're going to puke, and then plummets you two hundred feet into a death drop!

All I want is to get off this thing and get my life back.

I had no idea how I lost the money for my party!!

I was SO mad at myself!

While Zoey talked to the store manager to see if any money had been turned in, Chloe and I wandered aimlessly up and down the aisles of the store, trying to retrace our steps.

But it was hopeless! I couldn't believe we were going to have to cancel my party AGAIN.

I burst into tears right there in the store as Chloe and Zoey did their best to try to console me. . . .

CHLOE AND ZOEY, GIVING ME A BIG HUG!

Somehow we accidentally activated that stupid party hat, because it started blaring the "Happy Birthday" song again.

I was a little surprised when Chloe and Zoey started singing "Happy Birthday" to me. Although it was probably the SADDEST version I've ever heard, since both of them were pretty down in the dumps too.

They started out singing kind of soft and shy, but by the last line they were singing boldly and passionately with all their hearts, like it was a Katy Perry power ballad or something.

My BFFs did that to make ME feel better because they CARED! And when they finally finished, I had a huge lump in my throat.

"Thanks, guys! I'm SO sorry!" I sniffed. "I know you worked really hard to help me with this party. Honestly, you both were looking forward to it even MORE than I was. Then I ruined everything by losing the money!"

"Listen, Nikki! This should have been all about YOU and your special day!" Chloe said. "But we made it about US! We were too busy trying to impress people and become more popular so we'd get invited to parties! We really let you down."

"We've been selfishly treating this like a huge social event and not like a celebration for the kindest, sweetest, most supportive friend we've ever known! I guess we both just got caught up in all the excitement," Zoey explained.

"Will you please forgive us?!" they both asked.

"Of course I will!" I gushed. "You guys are the best friends EVER! I'll NEVER forget how much fun we had today. Especially when we were goofing off, riding around in that cart and—!"

"OMG! THE CART!!" we shrieked.

We dashed to the first cart and started digging like mad through our big pile of party stuff. And lying on the very bottom of the cart was $200 in cash!

It had fallen out of my pocket!

OMG! We were SO happy and relieved!

And since my party was BACK ON again . . .

. . . WE RUSHED TO THE CHECKOUT LINE
BEFORE WE HAD ANOTHER DISASTER!

Once we got back to my house, we placed all the bags in my bedroom.

Then we carefully reviewed our checklist.

We had the pool, food, birthday cake, decorations, party supplies, games, and DJ for the music.

Everything was all set for my party!

SQUEEE ☺!

After Chloe and Zoey left, I collapsed onto my bed in exhaustion.

I was happy, and it felt really good to FINALLY have my life under control.

Suddenly my cell phone beeped.

Then, a few seconds later, it beeped again. This meant I had just received two new e-mails. I glanced at them and groaned loudly. . . .

From	Subject
Trevor Chase	Your Itinerary for Bad Boyz Tour
Madame Danielle	Your Itinerary for Trip to Paris

JUST GREAT!

I had my life under control, all right!

For, like, thirty seconds!

☹!!

THURSDAY, JUNE 26

JUST GREAT ☹!

Now I have a HOT MESS on my hands!

But it's all MY fault!

I very STUPIDLY agreed to do the Bad Boyz tour AND the trip to Paris.

AT THE SAME TIME!

WHO does something like that but a TOTAL LOSER?!

I really need to let Trevor Chase know ASAP that I WON'T be going on tour.

But I'm totally DREADING it.

I feel so GUILTY because Chloe, Zoey, and Brandon will probably be DEVASTATED once they find out!

I'm the WORST friend ever ☹!

My party is in forty-eight hours, and time is running out.

I finally decided to put aside all my fears and BRAVELY tackle my BIGGEST problem head-on!

Ignoring this very serious matter could turn into a humiliating DISASTER at my party.

So I did what any girl would do who's STUCK with an ugly, saggy, scratchy black SWIMSUIT from the Water Safety section of PE class.

I rushed to the mall to shop for a chic and stylish NEW swimsuit for my birthday party!

PROBLEM SOLVED ☺!

Hey! I'M the BIRTHDAY GIRL! It's mandatory that I look SUPERcute!

Right?! . . .

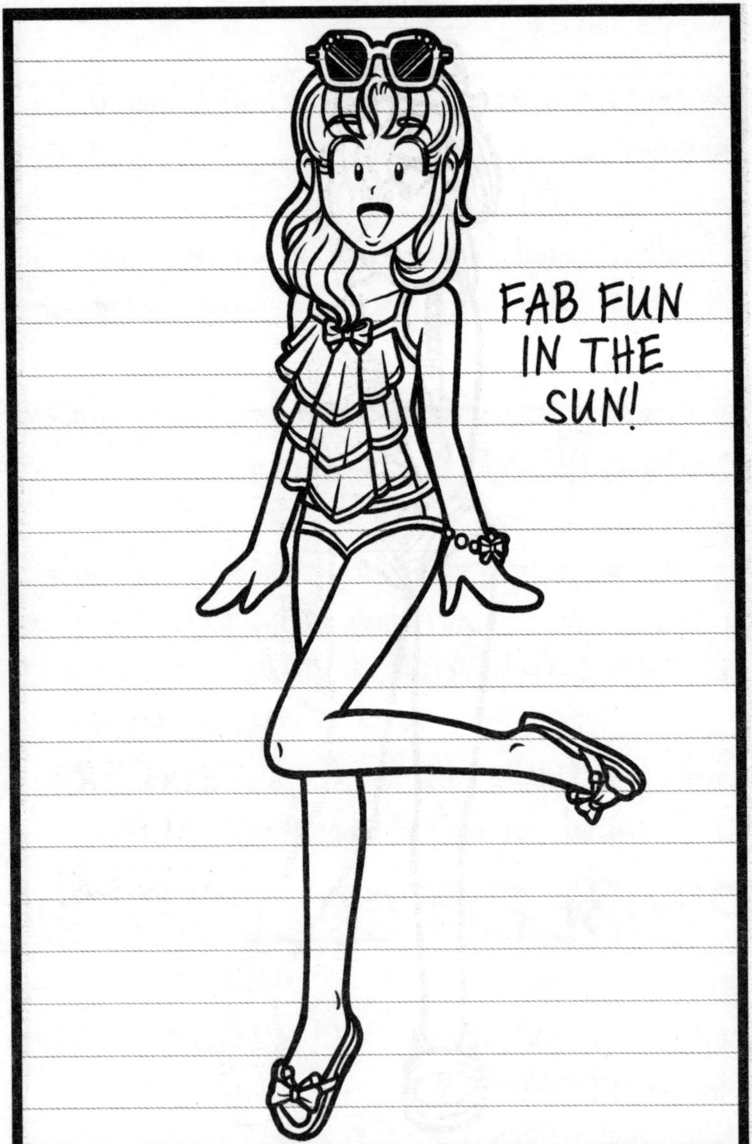
FAB FUN
IN THE
SUN!

SUPER
SURFER
GIRL
SUMMER!

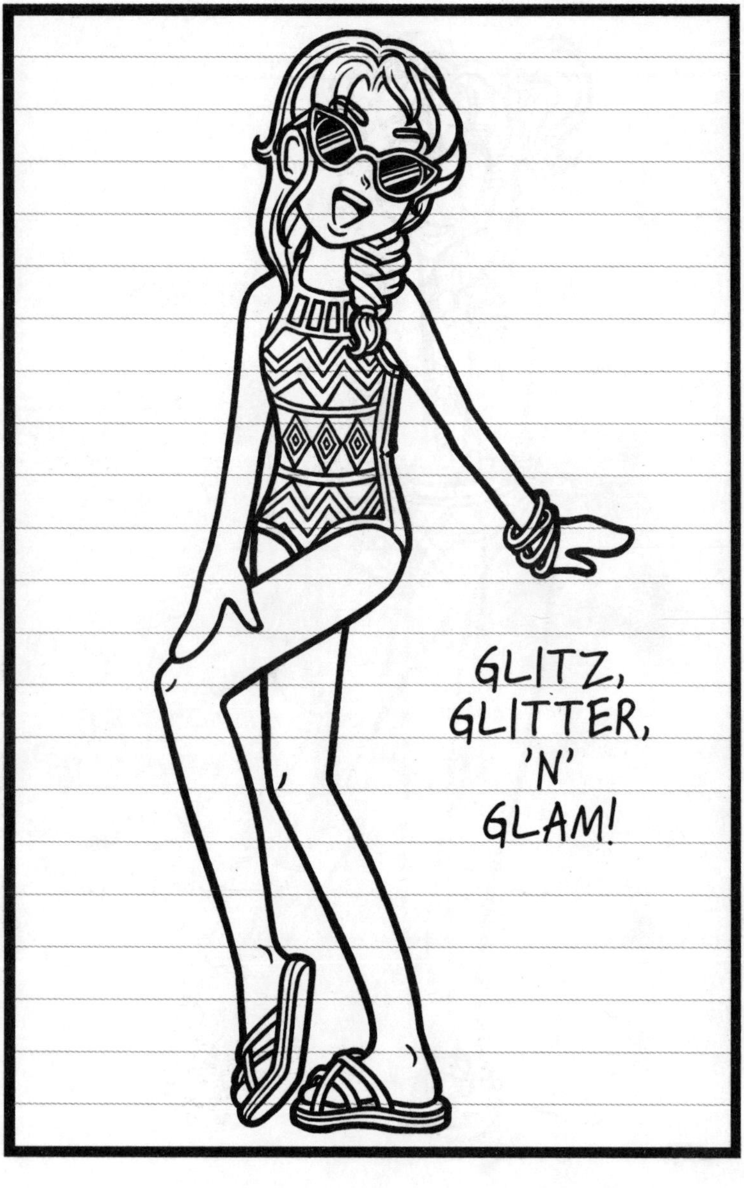
GLITZ,
GLITTER,
'N'
GLAM!

SPUNKY,
SPORTY
SPLASH
SPECTACULAR!

I loved ALL the swimsuits and had fun trying them on with various shoes and hairstyles.

Of course I sent selfies to Chloe and Zoey. They enjoyed my swimwear TRY-ON-A-THON and said I looked like a real fashion model.

We picked the Spunky, Sporty Splash Spectacular because tankinis are in!

I ALSO decided to DELAY the news about the Bad Boyz tour until AFTER my birthday party! I KNOW! I KNOW! My friends deserve to know my final decision. But it'll just spoil all the fun. The last thing I want is them moping around all down in the dumps at my birthday party.

Waiting a few more days won't really matter!

Like, WHAT could go wrong in just forty-eight hours?!

☺!

TOMORROW IS MY BIRTHDAY PARTY!!
SQUEEEE!!

I've gone through so much DRAMA this month, I honestly thought this day would NEVER come.

It feels like I've canceled this party one hundred times for some reason or another.

Chloe and Zoey are here now, so I gotta run!

The three of us and our moms are going to the pool this evening to start setting up for my party.

Then almost everything will be ready for tomorrow.

OMG!

I can't believe Brandon just texted me to say he's going to stop by to help out!

SQUEEEE!!

LATER! I'll write more tomorrow (if I get a chance)!

☺!!

SATURDAY, JUNE 28

OMG! My birthday party has been even more PERFECT than I'd imagined! It's been . . .

WONDERFUL ☺!!

I'm taking a quick break to write this so I'll remember everything FOREVER!! . . .

MY BEAUTIFUL BIRTHDAY CAKE
(WHICH CHEF BRI-BRI DID <u>NOT</u> BAKE)

ALL MY FRIENDS CAME TO MY PARTY!

A FEW OF MY FRENEMIES CAME TOO!

CHLOE, ZOEY, AND ME IN OUR SUPERCUTE
TROPICAL ISLAND OUTFITS

COOL ANDRÉ AND KA-RAY-ZEE MAX C.

HANGING OUT WITH MY FAMILY

273

Not only was my party a BLAST, but there were several MEMORABLE MOMENTS! . . .

MOST "VIRAL VIDEO" MOMENT

EVERYONE DABBING AND DOING COOL FORTNITE DANCES, LIKE THE FLOSS, HYPE, AND ORANGE JUSTICE!

MOST "PRINCESS SUGAR PLUM SUPERFANGIRL" MOMENT

VIOLET, CHASE, AND ME, TRYING TO RIDE
A UNICORN TO BABY UNICORN ISLAND
TO VISIT PRINCESS SUGAR PLUM!

CHEF BRI-BRI, CHARGING MACKENZIE
AND TIFFANY $25 TO EAT
FIFTEEN DOGGIE SNACKS!

BRANDON AND ME, TAKING A SELFIE!

What can I say?! My EPIC party is BANGIN'!

With all the confusion about whether my birthday party was ON or OFF, I never actually agreed to be either Brandon's or André's date.

So I was happy that they both came to my party and didn't SQUABBLE with each other like spoiled toddlers.

We all hung out together and had a lot of fun.

It was amazing that EVERYONE I invited actually came. I was SUPERexcited to see Brandon's good friend Max Crumbly, and my friend Chase, who I met when I was in the exchange program at North Hampton Hills.

And, as always, Violet totally rocked the house with her AWESOME DJ skillz and music.

I thanked Chloe and Zoey again for all their hard work and gave them a big hug!

This party NEVER would have happened without

THEIR encouragement and support. AND, of course, that AWESOME book they gave me, *My Very Rich and Trashy Life! Party Planner (Because Life's a Party and You Should Smile While You Still Have Teeth)!*

They're the BEST. FRIENDS. EVER!!

OMG! This was one of the HAPPIEST days of my ENTIRE LIFE!

SQUEEEEE!!

Anyway, I have to stop writing now. MacKenzie is being SUPERnice and wants to show me her birthday gift to make sure I like it. I guess inviting her WASN'T a huge mistake after all.

Hey! I'm just relieved she didn't RUIN my party like in that horrible NIGHTMARE!

☺!!

Okay, remember when I said that everything about my birthday party was PERFECT?

Well . . . I was WRONG ☹!!

And remember when I said I was just relieved MacKenzie hadn't RUINED my party like she'd done in that horrible nightmare?

Unfortunately, I was WRONG about that, too ☹!!

I should have been SUSPICIOUS when MacKenzie and Tiffany were acting really nice to me and gushing about how GREAT my party was and how I was going to LOVE, LOVE, LOVE the FABULOUS birthday present they got me.

And I should have been VERY SUSPICIOUS when they INSISTED that Brandon, Chloe, and Zoey come and see my fabulous present too! It was all just a sneaky plan to SABOTAGE my friendships! Because THIS is what happened! . . .

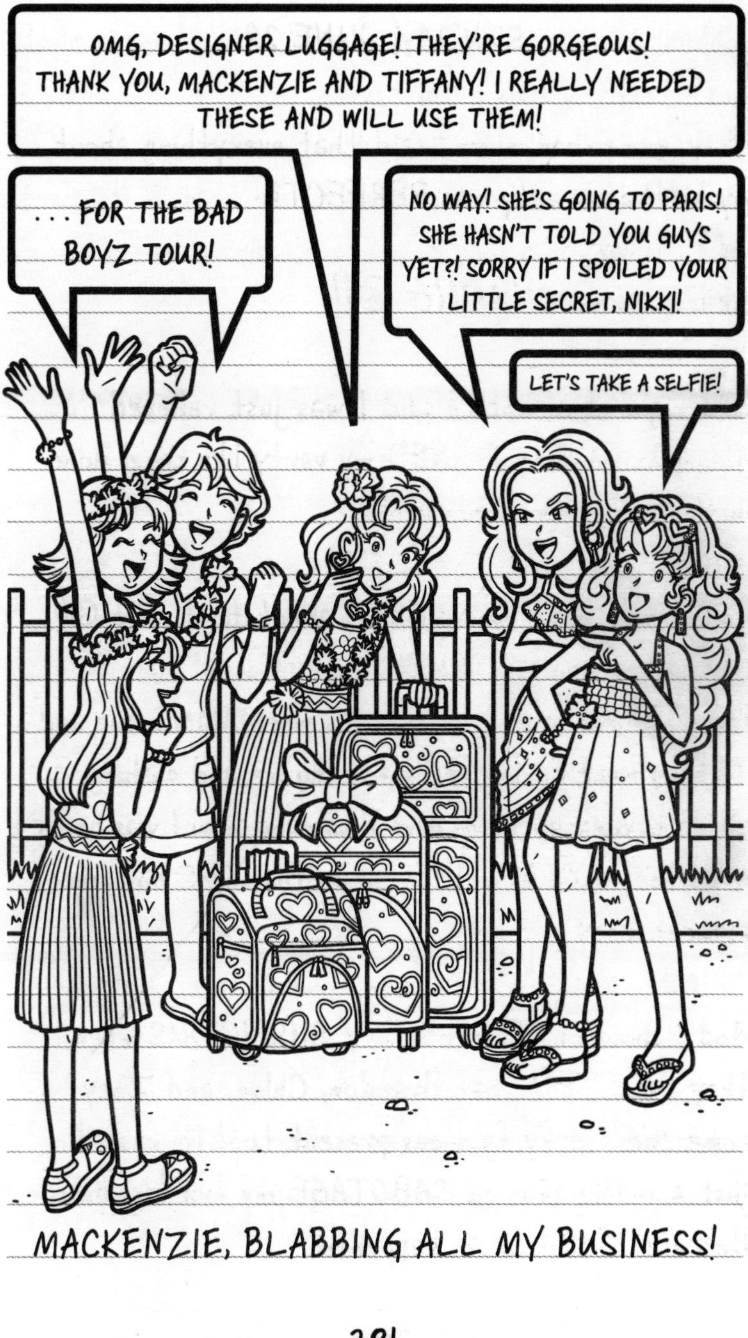

MACKENZIE, BLABBING ALL MY BUSINESS!

Chloe, Zoey, and Brandon just stared at me in shock with their mouths hanging open.

It was suddenly quite obvious to me that MacKenzie and Tiffany had only come to my birthday party to start some DRAMA!

Chloe glared at both of them. "You two are WRONG! If Nikki were going to Paris, she would have told us FIRST! We're her BFFs!"

"Sorry to burst your bubble! But not ALL the gossip you hear is TRUE!" Zoey fumed.

"Enough with the drama already!" Brandon sighed. "Nikki promised to tell us if she was going to Paris. And she would have IF it were true."

"RIGHT, NIKKI?!" my three friends asked suddenly, putting me on the spot.

"WRONG!" Tiffany sneered. "Nikki's name is on the list for the trip to Paris along with mine! I can show you the e-mail on my cell phone."

JUST GREAT ☹!! This was NOT the way
I wanted my friends to find out! I should've just
been honest and told them the truth weeks ago.

"Listen, g-guys! It's TRUE! I AM g-going to PARIS!"
I stammered nervously. Out of the corner of my eye,
I saw André standing nearby, and his face lit up with
a HUGE grin.

"YOU ARE?!" my friends gasped in disbelief.

"WHY didn't you tell us?!" Brandon asked.

"WHEN did you plan to tell us?!" Zoey asked.

"WHAT were you thinking?! You're going to Paris
with Tiffany?! Everyone knows that SHE HATES
YOUR GUTS!" Chloe scolded me.

Okay, my friends had just asked me WAY too many
COMPLICATED questions. "I planned to tell you.
Um . . . AFTER my party. But I was really worried
you guys would be upset or mad at me. So I kind of
procrastinated just a little," I muttered.

"Nikki, we're your FRIENDS! We're actually HAPPY for you! You didn't have to keep Paris a SECRET from us!" Zoey exclaimed.

"I DIDN'T?! Um . . . I mean, I DIDN'T! I'd NEVER do that!" I lied. "Keeping a secret like that from your best friends is really . . . SHADY!"

"Sure, we're a teeny bit DISAPPOINTED!" Chloe griped. "And maybe a little UPSET! And possibly TOTALLY DEVASTATED! But we'll get over it. Maybe!" . . .

MY TOTALLY DEVASTATED FRIENDS?!

"We just want you to achieve your DREAMS! Nikki, you deserve Paris!" Brandon gushed.

Then the strangest thing happened.

My friends started planning a BON VOYAGE party for me!

Right there at my BIRTHDAY party!

Like, WHO does THAT?!

My SILLY, WONDERFUL, ADORKABLE friends, that's who ☺!

I'm REALLY going to miss them ☹!

MacKenzie and Tiffany just smirked and rolled their eyes at us. I felt the OVERWHELMING urge to yell, "SHUT UP!" even though they weren't saying anything.

For weeks I'd been totally stressing about Paris and keeping it a deep, dark secret from my friends.

For no reason WHATSOEVER!

Well, one thing is for sure. I will NOT be inviting
those DRAMA QUEENS to my bon voyage party.

I have two words for each of them: "GIRL, BYE!"

☺!

MONDAY, JUNE 30

I barely got any sleep last night! I just tossed and turned for hours, my thoughts racing.

My party was a huge success! My friends are supportive! I co-own a booming doggie snack business with the world-famous child prodigy Chef Bri-Bri, pastry chef to the stars! And I have a SUPERexciting summer ahead of me!

But, deep down, something just didn't feel right. I wasn't sure WHAT it was or HOW to fix it.

I was pleasantly surprised when I got a phone call yesterday from my friend Chase. She said she'd had a great time at my party and had met a guy there named Max Crumbly. I told her all about him and that he's really nice. I couldn't help but gush about how they'd make a really CUTE couple ☺!

Chase and I had originally planned to be roommates for the trip to Paris. But it's just my ROTTEN LUCK that she ended up on the waiting list instead of that selfie-addicted drama queen, Tiffany ☹!

Anyway, later on I was chillaxing with my diary and procrastinating about writing the thank-you cards for my birthday presents . . .

. . . when I got a very STRANGE text from Brandon!

He said he had just gotten some really GOOD NEWS and that I needed to meet him at the CupCakery in ten minutes because he wanted to tell me in person.

TEN MINUTES?! WHAT was going on?!

I was pretty sure it was about Fuzzy Friends. Probably that fund-raiser I'd helped him with. He LOVES that place and is really passionate about finding good homes for the animals. It's just one of the things I really adore about him.

Suddenly I got a huge lump in my throat. OMG! I was ALREADY starting to miss him!

That's when I came up with a BRILLIANT plan.

First I made a couple of quick phone calls. Then I sat down and wrote a very special letter to Brandon. I pretty much poured my heart out.

When I arrived at the CupCakery, I was shocked and surprised to see that he'd written a letter to ME, too! So we exchanged letters. . . .

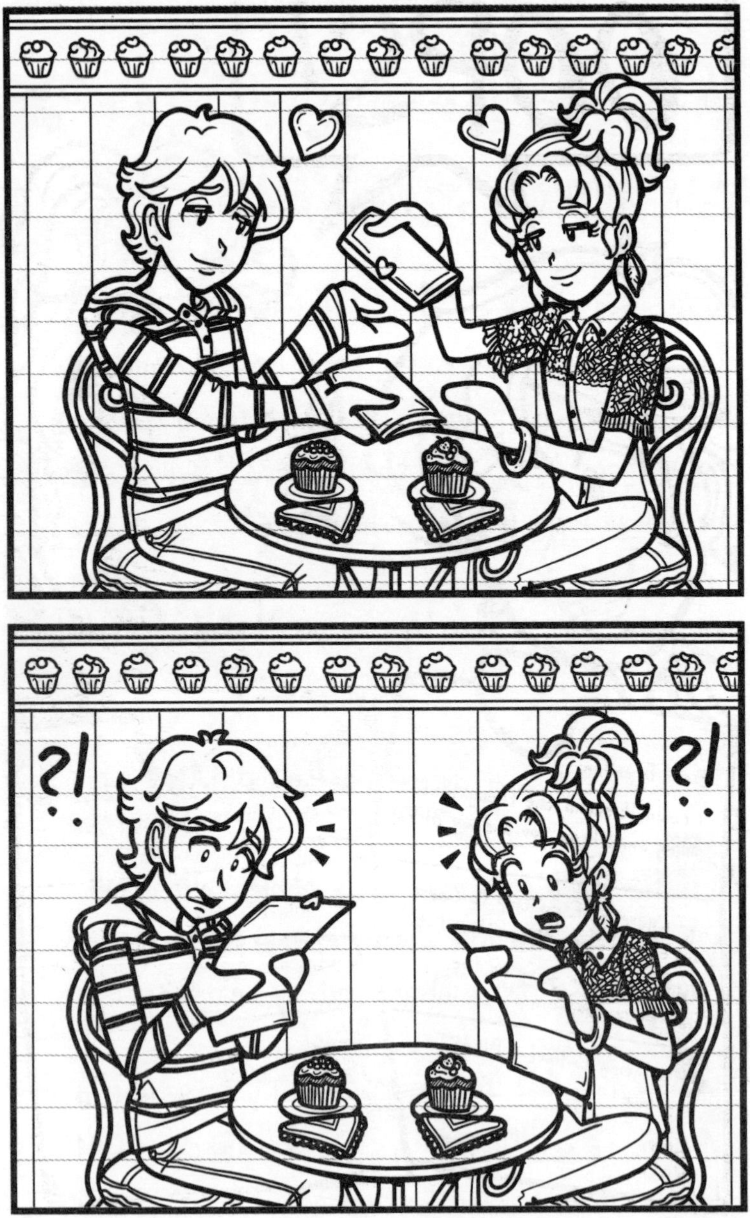
?!
?!

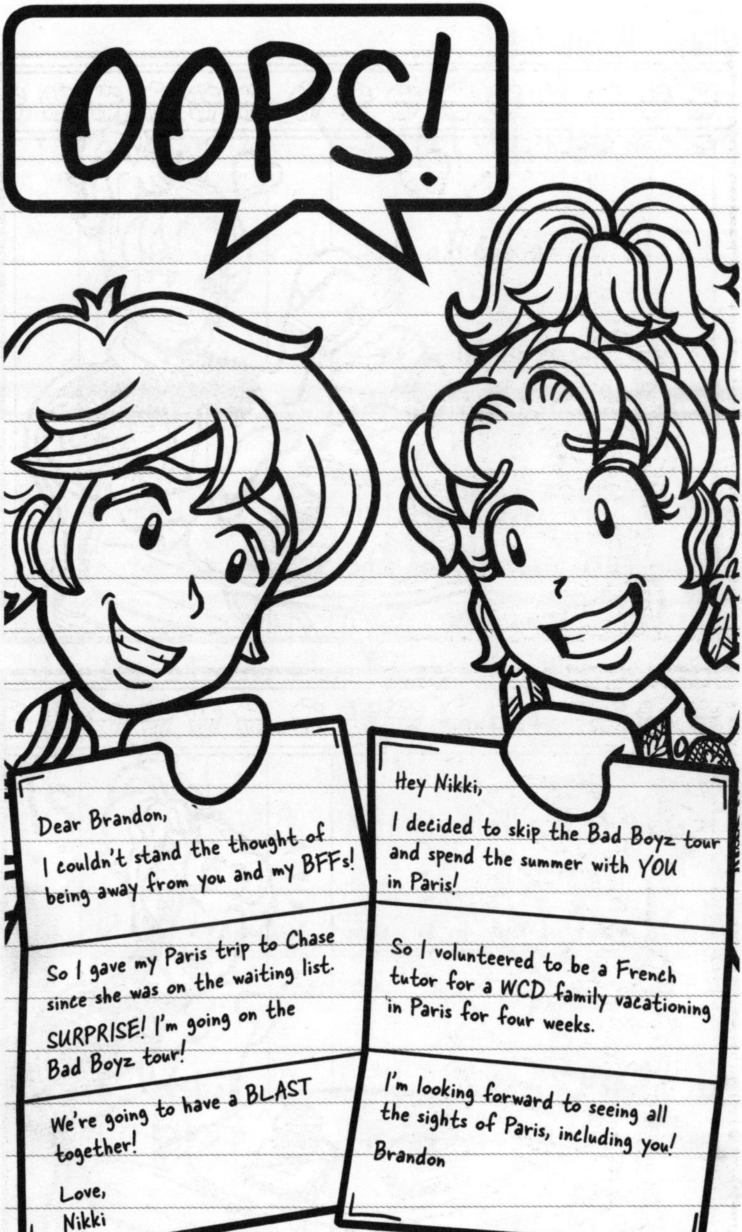
OOPS!
Dear Brandon,
I couldn't stand the thought of being away from you and my BFFs!
So I gave my Paris trip to Chase since she was on the waiting list.
SURPRISE! I'm going on the Bad Boyz tour!
We're going to have a BLAST together!
Love,
Nikki
Hey Nikki,
I decided to skip the Bad Boyz tour and spend the summer with YOU in Paris!
So I volunteered to be a French tutor for a WCD family vacationing in Paris for four weeks.
I'm looking forward to seeing all the sights of Paris, including you!
Brandon

Okay, I'll admit it!

Brandon and I TOTALLY MESSED UP!

At first we were both really UPSET!

The humongous problem we were trying to fix was ME in Paris and HIM on the Bad Boyz tour.

Instead, we'd just completely reversed things, with HIM in Paris and ME on the Bad Boyz tour.

Unfortunately, we were STILL going to be apart for most of the summer ☹!

Then we felt a little EMBARRASSED!

We had poured our hearts out and then rashly made sacrifices to try to be together.

Just like characters in some mushy, modern-day *Romeo and Juliet*—ish romantic . . . TRAGEDY.

And we felt really SILLY!

The entire thing had backfired and turned into a CRUEL joke! We were expecting a hidden TV camera to appear and for someone to yell, "YOU JUST GOT PRANKED!"

We sat there staring at each other in frustration. Until finally we smiled at each other, then snickered, then cracked up laughing until our sides ached. We had to admit that the whole situation was INSANELY funny!

It was quite obvious that Brandon and I REALLY like each other! A LOT!

SQUEEEEE ☺!

Anyway, since it would have been very RUDE to call Chase and demand that she give me back my trip to Paris, we decided that Brandon would try to find a replacement for his tutoring position.

Which, to be honest, shouldn't be that difficult.

Hey, MacKenzie speaks French, right?! I'd LOVE to

ship HER off to another continent for the rest of the summer!

She and Tiffany DESERVE each other.

Besides, WHO wouldn't want to go on an all-expenses-paid trip to spend the summer in BEAUTIFUL, EXCITING, GLAMOROUS . . .

PARIS, the City of Light?!

Well, okay! The REAL question is, WHO wouldn't want to spend the summer in PARIS other than . . .

ME ☺?!
SORRY!

I can't help it. . . .

I'M SUCH A DORK!!
☺!!

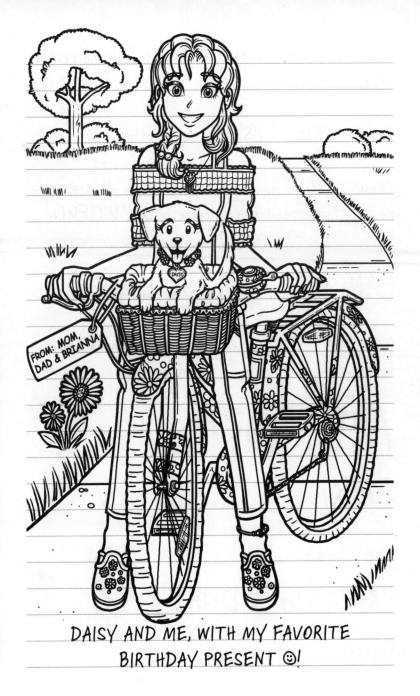

DAISY AND ME, WITH MY FAVORITE
BIRTHDAY PRESENT ☺!

Rachel Renée Russell is the #1

New York Times bestselling author of the blockbuster book series Dork Diaries and the bestselling series The Misadventures of Max Crumbly.

There are more than thirty-seven million copies of her books in print worldwide, and they have been translated into thirty-seven languages.

She enjoys working with her two daughters, Erin and Nikki, who help write and illustrate her books.

Rachel's message is "Always let your inner dork shine through!"